LEAVING
HOME

LEAVING
HOME

Storybook written by

Gail Hamilton

Based on the CBC TV series produced by
Sullivan Entertainment

WIND AT MY BACK

HarperCollins*PublishersLtd*

LEAVING HOME
Storybook written by Gail Hamilton

Copyright © 1997 by HarperCollins Publishers Ltd, and Sullivan
Entertainment International Inc.
Based on the CBC TV series produced by Sullivan Entertainment with
the participation of Telefilm Canada and with the assistance of the
Canada Television and Cable Production Fund - License Program and
with the assistance of the Government of Canada Canadian Film or
Video Production Tax Credit.

Based on the books *Never Sleep Three in a Bed* and *The Night We Stole the
Mountie's Car* by Max Braithwaite.
The characters and incidents portrayed are entirely fictitious. Any
resemblance to any person living or dead is coincidental.

Wind At My Back is the trademark of Sullivan Entertainment Inc.
Teleplay "Four Wall and a Roof Parts 1 and 2" written by Marlene
Matthews and Raymond Storey

http://www.harpercollins.com/canada
http://www.sullivan-ent.com/canada

First edition

Canadian Cataloguing in Publication Data

Hamilton, Gail
Leaving home

Based on the Sullivan Entertainment/CBC-TV series, Wind at my back.
ISBN 0-00-648149-3

I. Title.

PS8565.A5354L42 1997   jC813'.54   C97-930251-X
PZ7.H1816Le 1997

97 98 99 ❖ WEB 10 9 8 7 6 5 4 3 2 1

Printed and bound in Canada

CHAPTER ONE

The Great Depression of the 1930s hit the small northern city of North Bridge very hard. Hard enough to slow business to a crawl and cause a great many citizens to wonder where their next meal was coming from. Everyone learned to make do with whatever they managed to hang onto, patching and mending where necessary. There didn't seem to be any money anywhere to buy anything new.

None of this affected the high spirits of two boys racing through the hot summer afternoon. Playing tag, they sped up the Main Street of North

Bridge, past the battered automobiles, the weather-bleached awnings, the sidewalks cracking for want of repair. The next moment they clattered into the hardware store run by their parents, kicking up dust with their flying feet.

Hub was twelve, Fat was ten. The boys had real names but they rarely thought of them. They had been known as Hub and Fat ever since they could remember. Their mother, Honey, stood behind the wooden counter holding the baby of the family, two-year-old Violet, in her arms. Their father, Jack Bailey, tall and dark-haired, stacked paint cans and grinned at his sons as they tore past.

"Mom!" Fat shouted as he pursued his bother hotly. "Hub swiped the ring from my Cracker Jack box!"

"Whoa, whoa!" Jack called out indulgently. "Fellas ... fellas ..."

"I did not," Hub insisted. "He lost it."

The lads might have gotten into a scrap over it if Honey hadn't nabbed Hub as he ran for the door. Truth to tell, Hub sometimes teased his younger brother. And the more merciless Hub's teasing became, the more Fat stayed glued to his heels.

"Hub Bailey, go finish your deliveries."

Honey Bailey, a pretty woman in her early thirties, was aptly named. She had thick honey-blond hair and her skin was lightly golden from the sun. Both boys had brown hair, a compromise between Honey's and their father's.

"I'm finished. I'm going to see my friends, okay?" Hub called out over his shoulder. When Fat made to follow, he glowered at his younger brother. "And you're not comin' either, Fat! I don't want you embarrassing me with the guys." The screen door slammed behind Hub with a mighty bang to emphasize the point.

"WAIT UP!" yelled Fat, whose principal occupation in life was trailing after Hub and trying to do what his brother was doing.

Honey and Jack had to laugh. Jack, a friendly, easygoing man, joined Honey, his arm casually around her. They loved running the hardware store together and made sure the boys helped with the business too.

"Fat ..." Jack shook his head. "You're just asking for trouble!"

Hub was fast, but not fast enough to lose his brother. So Fat was still tagging along as Hub dodged behind a bakery truck and a fruit stand and disappeared from his parents' sight.

Hub, with his tag-along brother, met his friends at the most exciting place he knew—a place they were sternly forbidden by their parents to go—the railroad yard.

The yard was stark behind the rickety fencing the lads had squeezed through. Box cars, interspersed with empty passenger cars, parked on the rails, their metal baking in the sun. Weeds sprouted up between the ties. Gravel, glinting with bits of broken glass, crunched beneath boots. In the distance, a train whistle wailed, only adding to the dingy, dangerous-looking loneliness that made the place so enticing to the town boys.

The air of desertion was deceptive, though. What was really going on was a very rough game of cat-and-mouse between those who ran the yard and those who weren't supposed to be there. Freight trains were often the only means of transportation for hoboes, men so down on their luck that they had no homes. They lived by scrounging and they rode the freight cars from town to town in a desperate search for work. Since these men paid no fares and were in constant danger of getting crushed as they hopped on and off moving trains, the railroad did everything it could to get rid of them.

As Hub and his friends arrived, the freight manager was talking to a couple of railroad cops, burly men no one would want to cross. Two hoboes, attempting to slip away before they could be caught, darted out from behind a boxcar and scurried between another row of cars. The sharp-eyed cops spied them and gave chase. Just in time, the boys crouched out of sight behind a yellow caboose. They knew the cops weren't very happy about kids getting in their way—getting caught could only mean big trouble.

"Mom says we're not supposed to be hanging around the railroad track," Fat whispered nervously. "Let's get out of here, you guys."

"Do you always have to listen to what Mom says?" Hub demanded. Count on a pesky little brother to lose his nerve just when he needed it the most.

"No, but there's cops around here. We're gonna get in trouble. Hub, how come they're after those bums?"

"Quit following me," was Hub's answer. Another problem was that little brothers kept asking questions when they ought to keep their heads down and their mouths shut .

Fat kept at Hub's heels as the boys edged around the train caboose. He hadn't really been to the railroad yard before and he was alarmed and worried about the bums, who looked so dirty and so hungry.

"Are they gonna stick 'em in jail? Hang 'em? Hub? How come they call 'em bums?"

"Cause they gotta bum money offa people. Now shut up and go home."

The railroad cops were getting closer, sending the boys scurrying over another set of tracks to a boxcar with an open door. Hub peered inside, sizing it up as a place to hide out.

"Nobody in this boxcar. Come on, you guys, we'll climb inside and wait. One of 'em's bound to come along."

Hub hoisted himself inside. Instantly, a hand was clapped over his face, jerking him back into a corner. As the boxcar door slammed shut, the only sound was feet on gravel as the rest of the boys tore off in fright. A vagrant gripped Hub tightly. Others, behind him, equally desperate-looking, crouched in the dimness.

"You're gonna get one of us killed," the hobo grunted fiercely to Hub. "If we don't kill you first. This train leaves in five minutes. Get outta here and don't say nothin', if you value your neck!" If the hoboes could hide until the trail pulled out, they would be safe until the next stop.

Hub bolted from the boxcar as though shot from a cannon and raced after his friends.

"Hub, wait up!" was the familiar shout as Fat,

who had loyally stayed behind, now panted along trying to keep up.

One fleeing hobo scrambled up a ladder to throw himself flat on top of the train. The other one dodged out of sight of the railway cops, who were throwing open boxcar doors and peering underneath at the undercarriage.

Fat tripped and sprawled on the cinders. "Owwww," he groaned, clutching his scraped knees in pain.

Exasperated, Hub doubled back.

Fat looked up to meet the eyes of the second hobo, who was clinging to the rods under the car. As Fat's heart began to pound with fright, the sound of running railroad cops grew louder.

"Shh, don't say nothing" the hobo pleaded, pressing his ragged body as far up as he could, hoping to stay undetected until the train got going.

"Hey! You!"

A cop had spotted the fellow. In a panic, the hobo let go and rolled down towards Fat. Fat saw the man stagger halfway up, then fall again under a fearful blow from the cop's billy club. As the cop raised the club for a second whack, Fat came to life. The fight between the big bully and the half-starved hobo was dreadfully unfair. Without even thinking, Fat jumped up and screamed out, "Hey! Leave him alone!"

The hobo used the distraction to escape. The angry cop seized Fat instead.

"What're you kids hangin' around here for? You wanta end up like these outta work vagrants?"

"Up here ... there's another one!" The cop's partner had spotted the hobo on the train's roof.

Fat found himself thrust aside. The air was filled with the clatter of boots on steel as the cops took off up the ladder to give chase. Hub grabbed Fat and dragged him off at a run in the direction of town. Fat's scraped knee was bleeding copiously.

"Mom's going to kill us," Fat muttered when they were safely out of danger. "What'll ya give me to keep quiet?"

"A knuckle sandwich."

The boys raced down a Main Street darkened by signs of hard times. Stores were boarded up or stocked with only a few scanty goods. Veale's Dry Goods, once the place where the Baileys had bought their clothes, now sported a torn "Auction" sign peeling off its darkened window.

Rounding a corner, Hub and Fat ran smack into another scene—one that was becoming all too familiar in those hard-up times. It was their own

Uncle Joe chasing an unshaven fellow, who was clutching a cardboard suitcase and clattering down the fire-escape stairs from the rooming house. Joe owned the house, and one of his tenants was trying to slip away without paying his bill.

"Nobody stiffs Joe H. Callaghan!" their uncle was shouting. "You're gonna pay me last month's rent, deadbeat. Stop!"

But the fellow had too much of a head start. He threw something at Joe and vanished round a corner without handing over any of the money Joe badly needed to pay the bills.

Giving up the chase, Joe turned back to Hub and Fat.

"Rent rooms to guys without jobs, and this is what you get, boys." He picked up the paper bag the man had thrown at him. "Donuts?" He handed it to Fat. "Give 'em to your mom."

Joe, Honey's younger brother, was a boyish twenty-six. With fair hair and almond-shaped eyes, he looked a lot like his sister. Things had been pretty tough for Joe lately, but he never let anything get him down for long.

"Hey, Uncle Joe," Fat began, "we were down at the rail yard an' Hub caught a bum."

"Put a sock in it," Hub ordered, taking a half-hearted swing at his brother.

"Hey, hey! That's enough," chuckled Joe. "When are you guys gonna get along? By the way, have I ever told you my three rules to a happy life? Number one—pay the bank. Number two—pay the bank."

"What's number three?" Fat asked.

"Marry money. Now go on, get outta here. I'll see you at supper time."

"Thanks, Uncle Joe," called Fat as he took off after Hub once again. Fat had acquired his nickname early in life from his almost comical love of eating. The donuts were the best treat he could imagine!

Shortly, they reached the old brick building from which swung the sign that read "Bailey's Hardware, Est. 1922." The storefront was stacked full of washboards, tin tubs, saw blades and such. Like many of the stores in town, theirs had a sign stuck in the window: "All stock reduced." Hard times were squeezing this business, too.

The boys banged the door and dashed to the counter, where Honey was waiting on Mrs. Webster, an elderly woman nervously fanning herself with a rolled-up newspaper. It was a scorching day, and the lazy blades of the ceiling fan were having little effect on the heat. Honey juggled

Violet on one arm while Jack, up on a ladder, was getting a small electric fan down from the shelf.

"Mom! Uncle Joe says he's comin' for supper. And guess what we got!" Fat burst out. "Donuts! Can I have one? I'm starvin'."

Honey took immediate possession of the donuts. "No! You'll spoil your supper. And keep your voice down. Sorry, Mrs. Webster."

"Raised four of my own," Mrs. Webster returned wistfully. The kindliness in her face was etched over by worry lines.

Honey finished writing up the bill. "Okay, that'll be two dollars and fifty cents, please."

Mrs. Webster hesitated, embarrassed. "I can give you fifty cents now, and two dollars in a couple of weeks maybe. Ah ... Mr. Webster's been under the weather since he lost his job. Our place is hot as Hades."

Confronted by Honey's sudden frown, the woman fingered her purse awkwardly. This was the first time she had ever asked for credit here, and the effort cost her.

Jack handed the fan to Hub. "I hope Mr. Webster's on the mend real soon. Hub, take that for Mrs. Webster."

"Bless you, Jack," Mrs. Webster breathed gratefully. "We always pay our bills."

Hub carried the fan out of the store, with Mrs. Webster hurrying behind. Honey sighed and shook her head at her husband. More and more people wanted credit these days, and Jack was feeling sorry for them and letting them have it.

"Oh for Pete's sake," Jack exclaimed, "it's hotter than an oven out there. The old fellow's outta work. What are you gonna do—say sorry, can't sell you a lousy fan?"

"We've got two dozen customers who can't settle their accounts! Sooner or later they all go on Relief." "Relief" meant they were so broke they had to rely on handouts from the government.

"Like the hobo! Dad, we saw a hobo get beat up down at the train yard. You shoulda seen it!" Fat piped up, caught up in the melodrama of it all.

Hub came back just in time to hear his brother getting them both into trouble. "He's exaggerating!" he insisted. Trust Fat to blow the fact that they had been where they shouldn't.

"No I'm not. You almost got killed, Hub!"

Much to the boys' dismay, their mother forgot all about Mrs. Webster and turned her attention to her sons and their dangerous disobedience. "Did I not warn you boys? I've told you again and again to stay away from the train yards."

Hub glared at Fat. With their mother this angry, they could only imagine what kind of punishment they were in for!

CHAPTER TWO

Hub and Fat felt lucky—their mother simply shooed them upstairs to the family's apartment over the store, where they were to sit in their room and think about their misbehavior.

Later in the afternoon, they sprawled in front of the big Philco radio in the living room, which was the center of entertainment in those days before television. Guy Lombardo's orchestra was playing "Wrap your troubles in dreams, dream your troubles away."

Honey was finishing up a batch of plum preserves, the shining mason jars cooling on the counter. Hub read the comics in the paper while Fat played jacks. Honey glanced at Jack, whose head was bent over bills and account books at the kitchen table. Uncle Joe sprawled on the couch, bouncing Violet on his knee, who giggled with delight. The donuts, what was left of them, sat near a basket that held the plums.

"Well? How bad is it?" Honey finally asked her husband, who had been chewing his lip anxiously.

"Receivables are kinda piling up."

"Fat, turn the radio down, please!" Honey called over her shoulder before turning back to Jack. "I told you. You have to quit being such a soft touch."

"Now," mused Joe dreamily, "if I had a store ..."

"How about if you had a job," his sister commented tartly. Joe was known for his wild schemes and big dreams that hadn't, so far, made him rich.

"Well, I'm lookin', Sis. I gotta keep my mortgage payments up. Don't want my real estate to go to pot."

"Things are gettin' tougher everywhere." Jack sighed, trying not to think of the two dollars he had let Mrs. Webster put on credit. How could he have said no to such a familiar old customer?

"Oh, you got that right," Joe put in. "They're ridin' the rails up in Toronto, lookin' for jobs. Still got my properties, and I'm not on the dole." "Dole," like "Relief," meant handouts from the government.

"Because you mooch all your meals off us," Honey returned, half in exasperation, half in affection. She loved her brother dearly, but he did keep turning up at supper time.

Joe only grinned at her and winked.

Honey looked over Jack's shoulder as he wearily added up figures. Then Jack closed the book, glanced at Honey for a moment and lowered his voice so that the kids couldn't hear. "Bank manager called. He wants to see me."

"Oh great. What does he want?" Probably the most feared person in North Bridge was the bank manager.

Though Jack tried to be nonchalant, the children picked up on the tension immediately. All three of them, including young Violet, forgot about the radio and watched their parents with wide, serious eyes.

Jack shrugged. "Oh, you know. Banks have to balance the books same as us."

That was just what Honey was afraid of. "When bank managers want to talk, that means trouble. Look at Veale's Dry Goods. Came down on them faster than a fly-swatter, and they've closed other stores, too."

"Well, banks need customers. They can't close down the whole town."

"Oh yeah? Look at this." Honey pointed to the newspaper headlines. "'Drought out West, banks foreclose.' And this is moving across the country, Jack. You mark my words."

"I've got some good ideas to throw in front of them. You know, uh, I think the only way to compete these days is with major advertising. All the big chains do it."

"Jack ... we're not Eaton's." Eaton's had about the biggest chain of stores in the country.

"Radio rates are cheap these days," Jack argued, undaunted. "On a reasonable advertising budget, you could reduce stock and keep the bank happy."

"Well, they're not going to lend us another red cent."

Jack leaned back in his chair, and Fat came over and climbed into his lap.

"President Hoover says good times are just around the corner," Fat read from the newspaper—which failed to impress his mother.

"Don't believe anything you hear and only about half of what you read."

"Ah, Hoover just says that to keep the truth from people," Joe added, getting in his two cents' worth.

But Honey didn't care to argue about the American president. The only thing on her mind was dealing with their cash crunch. Unlike Jack, Honey came from a poor family, and she knew what could happen if you didn't have any money. She was much more of a hardheaded realist than her husband.

"We'd better start buttering up our suppliers."

"What do you know about Hoover?" Jack asked Fat to tease him. "What do you know about reading the paper? Stay away from papers. Papers will only cause you grief."

Fat giggled uncontrollably as Jack wrestled him into a hammerlock. Jack adored both his sons and both of them adored him back. For the moment, all was forgotten in some good old-fashioned rough-housing.

The next day, the boys carried out boxes of shingles for Owen Petrie, an old customer whose building business had been a mainstay of Bailey's Hardware. After they had finished loading the boxes into the back of Owen's truck, Owen waved to Honey and began to get into the cab.

"Be seeing you now, Mrs. Bailey. Sorry I missed Jack."

Hastily, Honey trotted after him and caught him before he could get the cab door closed. "Mr. Petrie? We aren't offering credit to our customers any more."

At the sight of the bill in her hand, Owen looked uncomfortable. "Look ... um, things are kinda tight ..." he began.

"They're kinda tight for us, too," Honey replied.

"Jack's over at the bank right now."

The boys peered through the screen door of the store, watching their mother take her stand.

"Boy, Mom's tough, eh?" Fat commented. "Too bad Dad ain't here. He'd give Mr. Petrie those dumb shingles."

Honey didn't back down—she just couldn't afford to. And she knew that Jack's generosity had become a big part of the store's problem.

"You don't pay us and we can't pay the manufacturer. We end up with empty shelves and a pile of bills."

Owen Petrie badly needed the shingles even though he didn't have the money. "This roofing job is gonna really put me right back in business ..."

Honey was saved from arguing with Owen by the arrival of her husband, back from the bank. His face was a queer ashen shade, but Honey didn't immediately notice. She only appealed to him to settle the problem with Owen.

"Give him whatever he wants," Jack flung out wildly. "Give him the whole bloody store."

"Jack ..."

Honey stared at him but he kept walking, looking unsteady as he went. In alarm, she ran after him, leaving Owen Petrie to drive away with the shingles.

Jack stormed into the store, swept a stack of paint cans violently from the counter and finally slumped down on the stairs leading up to the apartment.

"What happened?" Hub asked his mother, frightened to see his father like that.

"Not now ..."

Honey had no time to calm her sons as she sped through the store after her husband. She left Hub full of alarm and Fat trying to retrieve the paint cans. Neither boy had ever seen their father act in such a manner.

Honey sat down beside Jack, who now looked as though all emotion had been drained out of him.

"Damn! He called our loan. Just like that. He said, 'Jack, I'm sorry ...'"

"That can't be!" protested Honey, shocked. Her eyes wide, she tried to process the information. "What reason did he give?"

Jack noticed the boys, who had now crowded into the doorway. "Go lock up the store," he told them.

"But it's the middle of the day."

"JUST GO!" Jack roared, sending the boys scrambling. But they only went around the corner out of sight, not out of earshot. Hub strained to listen, afraid that something momentous was going on.

Jack dropped his head again and dragged one hand through his hair. "He threw my advertising plan back in my face. Said it's ... too late."

"Too late?" Honey croaked. Jack had gone off with such brave hopes.

"Some clerk at the wholesale place down south saw our accounts in the red. So he called Barret at the bank to see if we were still good for it. Barret immediately pulled the plug on us." The Baileys had no money to repay their bank loan. And with no money and no credit at the bank, there could be no hardware store.

Honey's face grew as white as Jack's as she contemplated the ruin of their lives. "I warned you about keeping our suppliers on our side. Well, I am not going to take this sitting down. I am going to give him a piece of my mind." Before Jack could catch her, she was storming wildly out the door.

"Honey!" Jack shouted after her. "You're just going to make a fool of yourself. Honey ... come back!" Honey's fighting spirit was one of the things Jack loved about her, but this was a fight she could not win.

Mr. Barret had the misfortune to be leaving the bank just when Honey steamed up, ignoring the honking car that narrowly missed her. Her honey-colored hair flew in the wind and her apron was askew.

"Oh, Mrs. Bailey. I'm just on my way to lunch," Barret said, speeding his walk.

Honey Bailey was raging now, her face heated, her eyes blazing. She accosted the banker sharply.

"How can you eat after what you've just done? We have been in business for ten years. The people of this town depend on us!"

"Look here, my good lady. I'm not prepared to discuss this on the sidewalk. Now, good day." Turning his back on Honey, Mr. Barret began walking quickly, trying to escape.

Honey chased him in a fury and blocked his way. "Don't you dare walk away from me, you narrow-minded, nasty little man!"

Barret, who was indeed short, overweight and pompous, now tried to scurry sideways. "I refuse to make a spectacle of myself in the street. The bank is not a charity, it's a business, and this is a business decision."

"What kind of business destroys other people's lives!" Honey was getting hysterical. "Jack has some really good ideas, but you won't even listen to him! We can improve things. I'm telling you ... we can ..."

Jack arrived and pulled her away before Honey could actually attack the unfortunate man.

"LET ME GO, JACK!" she shouted at her husband, fighting him off. "Let me ..."

Sobbing, Honey wrenched herself out of Jack's grasp and fled past staring neighbors back into the store, with Jack on her heels. Hub and Fat had run outside after their mother, but she darted right past them. Fat's lip was quivering. Hub kicked his toe hard against the curb, mortified.

"Nobody else's mom screams at the top of her lungs in the street."

The moment they got inside, Jack jerked down the shade covering the door. Honey was still racked with panic and anger. There, among the shelves of lampshades and rows of garden hoes, she turned to Jack, desperately trying to fathom how this disaster had happened.

"How could you let it get this far? I tried to warn you. Why is everything on my shoulders? The boys, the books, the house ..."

"Shh ... shh ... calm down," crooned Jack in an effort to soothe her.

"I'm sick to death of you and your *calm down*. I WILL NOT CALM DOWN! Your brother was right about you! He said you never paid attention to details and you don't!"

Hurt and scared, Honey could not help lashing out at the man she loved most. Jack shook his head, reeling from this stunning blow. The catastrophe sank in.

"It's over," he said. "We're bankrupt."

The Baileys had seen this happen all too often to families they knew—and it was a terrible fate.

"Don't you ever use that filthy, rotten word ..." Honey choked out—and then she collapsed, sobbing, into her husband's arms.

CHAPTER THREE

Bankrupt they were. The bank immediately closed the store and seized its assets, including every bit of stock it had.

Jack began the heartbreaking rounds of looking for a job. Hat in hand, he went from business to business without success, often accompanied by Hub. He even tried Mr. Pappas, the paunchy owner of the Greek lunch counter at the train station.

"Sorry, not enough work for myself," Mr. Pappas rasped as he took in Jack's barely concealed desperation. "I can, uh, give you a bowla soup, maybe, you an' your son ..."

Mortified, Jack fled.

Ready to take a job as any kind of common laborer, he tried the North Bridge Nickel office next. Clean shaven and neatly dressed, he found himself standing around in front of the office with a horde of gaunt, shabby men, including several hoboes like the ones Hub and Fat had seen at the railroad yard. As the office door opened, a shiver of hope went through the men. Jack pushed forward.

"Nothing today, boys," the official announced, and he slammed the door again.

Life seemed to drain out of the little crowd. Wordlessly, the line broke up and the men dispersed. Hub ran to his father's side and fell into step beside him. This bankruptcy was perhaps hardest of all on Hub, who shrank inside at each blow to his father's pride.

Fat also worried about the future. That very night, Fat lay in bed in the apartment listening to his parents arguing in the next room. Hub, in the next bed, was fast asleep.

"Oh Jack, what are we going to do?" Honey asked in a strained, weary voice.

There was a significant pause. "I've called Mother. We're moving to New Bedford," Jack finally said, as though each word cost him a drop of blood to utter.

"Are you out of your mind?"

In spite of their desperate circumstances, Honey was horrified. Jack came from a prominent mining family in New Bedford headed by his widowed mother, the imperious and intimidating May Bailey. Jack had had a dreadful falling-out with his mother over his decision to marry Honey Callaghan, whose background was too poor and unpolished and Irish to suit Mrs. Bailey. Mother and son had barely spoken since. The fact that Jack had actually appealed to her for help showed how far he was willing to swallow his pride to save his family.

"Honey, we can't live in the streets. The auction is tomorrow. We have to think of the kids first."

Though Jack sounded defeated and at his wits' end, Honey's own pride was stung. "Moving there is not going to solve our problems," she insisted hotly. "That woman despises me." May Bailey had made no secret of her opinion of Honey .

In the bedroom, Fat scurried over to Hub's bed and shook him by the shoulder. "Hub, Hub! Wake up, wake up! We're leaving North Bridge and moving to New Bedford."

This news was enough to jolt Hub wide awake. "Why?" he demanded, blinking the sleep from his eyes. The thought of leaving their familiar home was scary and momentous. Neither of the boys had actually thought of it before.

"He called Grandmother." Fat was already on the verge of tears. "I don't wanta live at her house. I don't even know her."

But Hub had seen his father scrounging for work, any work, and tried to be practical. "Maybe she can get Dad a job."

Just then another terrifying possibility struck Fat. "Hub, does this mean no more store?" Up until then, Fat had not grasped exactly what bankruptcy meant for the family.

"Well, what d'ya think it means?" Hub shot back.

"Maybe he'll open another one?"

"Where's he gonna get the money for another one, Fat?"

"I don't know. You don't have to be mad at me."

Fat was scared and needed his older brother's reassurance. Hub sighed. "Look, go to sleep, okay, Fat? We can't make it any harder for them. We gotta listen to what Dad says."

Hub scrunched up a pillow in his arms, as though it might shield him from his own fears. Fat lay staring at the ceiling. It was a very long time before either boy went to sleep.

In bankruptcy, the bank seized every last thing a person owned and then auctioned the property off, in an effort to reclaim as much money as possible. All too soon, Bailey's Hardware had big signs plastered all over its windows proclaiming "AUCTION TODAY."

The auctioneer set up in front of the store, and even though the day was blistering hot, a crowd came to get a good look at the items up for sale. When a hardware store went bust, there was bound to be plenty of useful stuff, if folks could only scrape up some change to buy it.

Honey, holding baby Violet and accompanied by her longtime neighbor, Mrs. Emans, watched numbly from the side. What Honey was staring at was the china currently in front of the auctioneer, a very beautiful set with rose garlands ornamenting its edges. The auctioneer held up a plate so all could see.

"We now have up for offer this fine eight-piece setting of Bridal Wreath pattern china. Who'll be offering...?"

"It's my mother's china," Honey moaned softly, sickened by the sight. Her mother hadn't had much to pass on to her daughter, but the china had been her proudest gift.

"Honey, I got two dollars. I'll bid on it," kindly Mrs. Emans told her impulsively. "Then you can buy it back when you save up the money." She waved her hand at the auctioneer. "Dollar and a quarter."

Honey looked at Mrs. Emans with sudden, grateful tears in her eyes. The auctioneer acknowledged Mrs. Emans, then spotted someone else upping the bid.

"Dollar fifty ... do I hear seventy-five...?"

"Two!" called out Mrs. Emans, blowing all her reserves at once.

"I have two, I have two," the auctioneer intoned—and for a moment Honey's face quivered with hope. "Do I hear two and a quarter?"

Mrs. Emans shot an elated glance at Honey. Then another bidder's hand, offering that extra, fatal quarter, squelched Honey's hope cruelly.

Inside the store, the shelves were almost barren of stock, making the place look strange, sad and very empty. Hub and Fat stood near the front door watching the last of the contents being hauled outside by the auctioneer's helpers. Fat's face was the very picture of misery, and Hub's wasn't much better. They, too, eyed the china that had graced Sunday dinners for as long as they could remember.

"Let's go," muttered Hub. "I can't stand to watch."

It's a good thing they didn't watch. The auctioneer waved Honey's plate around for a final time and sold the set for two and a half dollars.

Mrs. Emans cast a defeated look at Honey, even as Honey watched her beloved china being carried off by a wart-nosed stranger, no doubt a dealer, smirking at his bargain.

"Oh well," Honey choked, heartbroken. To make matters worse, the auctioneer was now holding up a jar of the plum preserves Honey had just made a short while ago, when her home and business had still been intact.

Unable to stand it any longer, Honey fled inside the store, where almost nothing was left but dust and bleakness. There's no telling how long she might have stood there if she had not been roused by a dreadful squawking in the back yard. One glance out the window sent her bolting outside in outrage. Honey kept a few chickens so that her family could have eggs. The butcher from the next street over was in the chicken pen and in the

very act of wringing the neck of her favorite
Leghorn hen. Several other hens already lay dead
on the ground. Those still alive fluttered and cack-
led in terror.

"You've got the nerve of a canal horse!" Honey
shouted, seeing her darlings being massacred.
"Get the heck out of here!"

"Now hold on, Mrs. Bailey!"

Overwrought, Honey flew at the man, clawing
and hammering with her fists. The noise brought
Jack, Joe and the boys running.

"Haven't you got any common sense in that
thick skull of yours?" Jack roared at the butcher as
he pulled Honey off.

"I'm only takin' what's mine, Bailey," the
butcher retorted, feeling the sting of a long scratch
across his face. "Now call off your wife or I'll call
in the police."

The butcher was within his rights. He had just
bought the chickens from the auctioneer and
meant to have them all ready to sell as dinners as
soon as he could.

Honey ended up in a fury of anger and tears,
with Violet shrieking in her arms, as the boys led
her away to a neighboring veranda. Mrs. Emans
helped Honey up the stairs.

"Come on over here. You mustn't get yourself

all worked up," Mrs. Emans said as soothingly as she could. "There's no point, there's just no point at all. Sit down ..."

"I've nothing to feed my family. Nothing," Honey moaned in a dazed voice as she tried to soothe Violet. She didn't even have a dish left, never mind food.

While the boys stood by, stricken and helpless, Jack tried to console his wife by hugging her and patting her back. "We'll be all right ... it'll all work out. It will, it will. It'll all work out, you'll see."

Seeing how upset she was making everyone, Honey made a heroic effort to get a hold of herself. She recovered enough to grip Jack's hand.

"Go see what's left. I'm gonna be all right."

Chapter Four

When the auctioneer had finally finished his work, there was nothing left for the Baileys to do but leave. In the bare apartment, the family waited for Jack's brother to drive them to New Bedford. Honey perched on a trunk with Violet in her arms while Hub sat on the carpetless floor.

"Go and wash your face," Honey said to Fat.

"Just because we're poor doesn't mean we have to look poor. Go to the bathroom too, please." Honey turned her attention to Hub. "How 'bout you too, Hub."

"I already went." Hub gazed over at where the big Philco radio used to sit and remembered all the happy times the family had had around it. "I'm not even sure why we're going. I hardly know Grandma Bailey."

"Blood is thicker than water," muttered Jack gloomily, turning from the window and bracing himself for what were sure to be very rough waters ahead.

The honk of a car horn sent the boys dashing to the window.

"He's here! Uncle Bob is here!" Fat cried, peering through the glass. "Wow! It's a brand new Buick. What's Uncle Bob like, anyway?"

"I once heard Mom say he was a horse's rear end," Hub replied, luckily quietly enough that he wasn't overheard.

Bob quickly hoisted the carton containing Hub's and Fat's few things into the car. Bob was not as good-looking as Jack, though the family resemblance was there. But he was certainly much better dressed. In fact, with his bit of a paunch and his gleaming Buick, he presented an air of complacent affluence sharply at variance with the times and Jack's near destitution.

When Honey, Jack and the baby issued, for the last time, from the store, Bob held out his arms to Jack.

"There he is—that brother of mine! How are ya, pal, ol' pal?"

Jack managed a strained smile as Bob pumped his hand solidly. "Thanks for coming, Bob." Bob had never had a problem jumping at their mother's beck and call. Needless to say, the rebellious Jack did not get on well with such a brother.

"Hey, don't I always bail you out, kid?"

"Not always ..."

Bob ignored this and turned to Honey. "Oh there she is! Miss Canada, 1932. How are you, Honey?" He kissed Honey and swung Violet high in the air. "And who's this little doll? Come here, cutie, give Uncle Bob a kiss. Wait till your Aunt Toppy gets a load of you." Toppy was Bob's wife.

Hub and Fat came bounding out, excited to see this uncle they hardly knew.

"Hello, boys," greeted Bob. "How ya doin'? Jump right into the car, right there. I hope your shoes are clean."

"Nice to see you, Bob," smiled Honey. "It's been a long time."

"Well, lotta water under the bridge, Honey. Only in your case, it's a bit of a flood. Well, let's load up the jalopy everybody. Long road home."

Just then Joe hurried up to say goodbye. Honey turned to him, choking back tears. For a moment, neither of them could find words.

Joe hugged his sister. "I'll be up to see ya. Bring you some donuts if you're good." Joe chucked Honey under the chin and shepherded her into the car.

Jack shook Joe's hand. The manly handshake dissolved into a hug, as Bob settled in behind the wheel. Everyone piled in and waved as the heavy car started up. Finally Joe stood alone, watching as the car, and his sister's family, his only relatives in the world, pulled away.

Chrome catching the sun, the Buick headed north through terrain that became rockier by the mile. Despite all the windows being wide open, heat glanced off the metal and built up inside. Violet was fussing, and Fat lay limply with his head back against the seat.

"I feel sick," he bleated weakly.

"Shh ..." said Honey, tired and irritated. "Take some deep breaths. In ... out ... in ... out ..."

The car was indeed crowded and stifling.

Uncle Bob kept casting worried glances at Fat, who was leaning queasily against his mother. Honey tried to fan Fat with a newspaper.

"Look here, Honey," Bob said, concerned both for Fat and for the car's spanking new upholstery, "if he's feeling punk, let's just pull over right now."

Honey looked down at her son. "You gonna make it okay, Fat?"

Honey fanned Fat harder. Fat, quite green around the gills, nodded, sucked in his breath and stared fixedly out the window. They passed a few haggard hitchhikers, some carrying signs that read "Out of Work" and "Work for Food."

Bob glanced at these down-and-outers with contempt. "That's where our taxes go, folks. Buncha good-for-nothings. You sure don't want to end up like them, eh fellas? Lotta the idle are moving north to New Bedford, too. Hanging around the train yards. Mother always says, if a man really wants to find a job, he'll find a job."

"Yeah? When did Mother last look for work?" Jack snorted.

Bob shot his brother a warning glance. "You just do yourself a favor, Jack, don't talk that way at dinner."

"Don't worry, we're not staying for dinner."

Bob was taken aback. "You kidding me? Mother's expecting you."

"Ah ... Jack ... maybe we should," put in Honey, not wanting to offend her powerful mother-in-law.

"I told you, we're not," Jack replied firmly. "We're gonna stop in, say hello, and then we're gonna head for the lake."

Mrs. Bailey had offered Jack's family the use of the old summer cottage by the lake, unopened for years now and in goodness knows what kind of repair. The quicker Jack could get to it, the less time there would be for a royal blow-up with his mother.

"Mother is not going to take kindly to that, Jack," shrugged Bob. "But you go on, do what you want to do. You always have."

"Mommm ..." a quavering voice broke in, "I think I'm gonna ..."

Fat suddenly retched and threw up all over the seat, the floor and Honey. Hub gagged at the sight of his brother vomiting.

Bob glanced back in horror. "Oh no! Oh no! Please! Not in my brand new car!"

"YECCH! GET ME OUTTA HERE," shrieked Hub. "HE'S MAKIN' ME SICK!"

In the next moment, Hub started throwing up too.

"JACK! STOP THEM!" Bob cried to his brother in outrage. "For Pete's sake, can't you control your own kids?"

"Shut up, you jerk," Jack volleyed back. "It's not their fault. It's the lousy way you drive!"

Amidst a great screech of tires, the Buick lurched over to the side of the road, too late to save itself from carsick children. Hub and Fat wailed, Violet screeched, and they all tumbled out into the blistering summer sun.

During this enforced stop the Bailey family tried to recoup. Honey spread a blanket out in the grassy field beside them and set out their picnic of hard-boiled eggs, bread and butter. While she tried to clean up Fat, Jack peeled an egg. When Fat began to feel a little better, he lay down with his head in his mother's lap. Hub sprawled nearby, still green and queasy and more than a bit embarrassed. At twelve, he felt he really was too old to get sick in a car.

Bob, his face screwed up in distaste, was wiping off the soggy seat with a crunched-up wad of newspaper. All the car doors were open wide in an attempt to air the vehicle out.

"You never get a smell like this out," Bob complained, wincing at what his wife, Toppy, and daughter were going to say about it. Then he noticed Fat reaching for a hard-boiled egg.

"Don't let him eat eggs, for pity's sake! He'll upchuck all over again."

"I'm still hungry, Mom," Fat was always ready to eat, no matter how he felt.

"Shh ... Uncle Bob's upset." Honey turned to her brother-in-law, determined to keep the peace. "Bob, it was nice of Toppy to make us this lunch."

Wiping his hands, Bob crossed to join them, mollified. "Well heck, you know Toppy. Heart of gold. She's not as bad as you think she is, Honey."

"I never said that ..."

"You don't have to. She knows exactly how you feel about her."

"She wouldn't come to my wedding. How does she think I'd feel?"

When May Bailey decided to disapprove of Honey, she ordered the family to boycott the wedding, something a bride was not likely to forget—especially a spirited bride like Honey.

"Honey," Jack rumbled warningly.

"He brought it up, Jack. I didn't."

"No, no," interjected Bob. "Let her get it off her chest, Jack. Better now than in front of the women."

"God forbid they should hear the truth." Honey could feel her dander rising and struggled to stay calm. "How is my dear mother-in-law?"

"Well, she's fine, she's just fine," Bob answered. "She just had her sixty-fifth birthday and she's still going strong. And looking forward to seeing all of you, I can tell you."

Honey doubted that very much. "I just bet she's got that red carpet rolled right down the driveway."

Jack frowned. He was pretty worried about this unhappy homecoming. To say he didn't get along with his mother was an understatement.

"How's she taking it, Bob—me and Honey and the kids coming back?"

"Oh, I steer clear of those kinda subjects, Jacko," replied Bob. "It's Toppy who speaks to her every day, you know, church meetings and that sort of thing. I'm telling you those two, they get along like two peas in a pod."

As Honey shot Jack a look, Bob expanded with pride. "And of course Doris being her only grand-daughter ... well, as you can imagine, the sun rises and sets on her. You and Doris should get along just swell, Hub. Doris is a real whippersnapper at school. How about you two?"

"We're okay," Hub muttered noncommittally. Hub's school record, to tell the truth, was not exactly shining.

"Yes, well, we've got a fine school in New

Bedford, real fine. Your Grandma Bailey gives a scholarship every year."

Bob salted and munched on an egg. With studied casualness, he avoided his brother's eyes as he approached a very touchy topic.

"Um ... by the way, Jack, Mother's authorized me to offer you a job at the mine. I figure you're in no position to turn it down."

This was definitely not the right thing to say to a brother whose pride was already smarting badly from a business failure.

"Well, you figured wrong!"

"You be reasonable, Jack. This is no time to get uppity with her."

Now Jack really began to bristle. "I can imagine the kind of job you two have in mind for me. It's one where I take orders from you, right?" This was something Jack would never be able to abide, one of the reasons he had left New Bedford long ago.

"It's a job, Jack, it's a job! Now please don't bring this up at dinner tonight or there's gonna be heck to pay."

"I'm not staying for dinner. I told you that."

Bob flung down the napkin he had picked up, truly angry now. "What a bloody fool! I'm telling you, Jack, it's you! It's not mother, it's you. It always has been."

Bob stomped off back to the car. They were not even halfway to New Bedford yet and already a family fight loomed.

Fat and Hub, who had been listening to all this in pained silence, exchanged worried glances before piling obediently back into their seats to resume a journey that was now even more uncomfortable than before.

CHAPTER FIVE

Since Jack and Bob had nothing more to say to each other, a thick silence reigned in the car the rest of the way towards New Bedford. Nevertheless, a kind of excitement began to rise in the boys as the car turned down the road to town. All around were rolling hills drenched in sunlight and yellow buttercups. Stands of trees crested the hills. Weathered barns were being filled with sweet-smelling hay and green fields among the rock outcroppings made the land seem a summer paradise. The car crested a broad knoll and a cluster of buildings appeared before them.

"Here we are, folks," Bob announced, "good old New Bedford. There's the office, boys."

The car rolled past an enormous sign that read "Silver Dome Mines, A Division of Bailey Holdings." The sign was affixed to a large wooden structure with a metal roof and all the roughness of mining in its look. Behind it, machinery, other wooden buildings and heaps of broken stone indicated that the mine was alive and operating. Not far beyond, the short, narrow main street of New Bedford appeared, with a number of small stores peppering the central stretch.

After North Bridge, Hub was disappointed. "Gee, it's kinda small. What's there to do here?"

"Plenty, if you've got some get-up-and-go. In case your father didn't tell you, your grandfather was a pretty big person hereabouts. He founded this place when he struck silver forty years ago."

"I never knew that," Fat piped up, his eyes wide with wonder. "How come you never told me that, Dad?"

After the break with his mother, Jack had spoken of New Bedford as little as possible. He'd wanted an independent life, standing completely on his own, not trading on his family's prominence.

"Because Bob's in charge of boasting in our family," Jack said through his teeth.

"That's uncalled for, Jack. I'm proud of what our dad accomplished." Besides, Bob owed his good clothes and new car to the mine, which he managed for his mother. May, herself, had run the mine for years after her husband had been killed in a mining accident.

Silence set in once more until the car climbed up a hill overlooking the town and finally stopped in a broad gravel driveway.

"Grandma Bailey's!" Bob announced "Home sweet home sweet home."

Hub and Fat tumbled out of the car and, for one long moment, stood in awe. May Bailey's house was enormous and austere, with a grand, white-pillared porch. Its red brick walls were softened only by wisteria blossoms, and vines enclosed part of the veranda that ran all round. Great leafy trees shaded the broad lawn and well-kept shrubbery. The only note of dissonance was a battered old truck parked well off to the side.

As Jack helped Honey from the car, the only sign of life about the place was the movement of a lace curtain at one of the upstairs windows. A pair of steely eyes and a glimpse of gray hair were the sole indications that Grandma Bailey had noticed the arrival of her son's family. Her eyes, in an expressionless face, met Honey's for a moment, then the curtain dropped back. Not what anyone would call an enthusiastic welcome.

"Well come on, everybody." Bob, hearty once more, was hauling the suitcase out of the car. He nodded towards the old truck and laughed. "That truck's for you, Jack. Borrowed it from the shop. I know she looks like a bit of an old clunker but she's got a few miles left on her." The suitcase and the cartons were tossed into the back of the truck.

Suddenly the door burst open. Toppy Bailey and her daughter, Doris, came running out. Toppy was a plain, fortyish woman dressed in the best style New Bedford had to offer, with dark hair pinned in side rolls.

"Hello, sweetheart!" Bob greeted his daughter fondly.

"Daddy!"

"Well, you say hello to your Uncle Jack and Aunt Honey," Bob instructed. "And I bet you don't even recognize your little cousins. Hub here, he's almost ready for shaving!"

This embarrassed Hub immediately, and his reaction was to jut out his jaw and glower balefully at Doris through the strained hellos all round. At fourteen, Doris was a tallish, fair-haired girl dressed with excruciating neatness, whose expression indicated a high opinion of herself.

"Jack and Honey!" Toppy exclaimed. "If you

aren't a sight for sore eyes!" Then her nose wrinkled. "Ewww ... what is that awful smell?"

"I'm afraid the boys had a little—"

"Oh no!" Toppy cried, cutting off her husband. "Not in our new car! Bob, I warned you to take the truck."

Before Toppy could say more, a younger woman of about thirty came flying out of the house. Her face was alight with happiness—a happiness that warred with a kind of guilty uncertainty about being so wildly pleased to see someone. This was Grace, Jack's unmarried younger sister, the one stuck living at home with her mother. She stood frozen for a moment. Then, unable to contain herself any longer, she flung out her arms.

"Jack!"

"Grace!" Jack spun around, his face, like hers, transformed with joy. He scooped his sister up and swung her round and round. Grace's face went pink with delight.

"Jack Bailey! You put me down!" she giggled, not meaning it in the least.

Jack gave her a final whirl before looking her up and down.

"Look at you! God, it's so good to see you, Grace. Where's Mother?"

"She's inside. She's probably waiting to make

her grand entrance." Grace had lowered her voice to a whisper, as though Grandma Bailey could hear through the walls.

Grace turned to smile at her sister-in-law. "Honey, I'm awfully glad you're here. And the boys. Goodness, how they've grown. Come on inside. Mother's got dinner on the table. She'll be pleased you're right on time. Come on boys, say hello to your grandmother."

Grace hurried back to the house, smiling at Jack over her shoulder. Hub and Fat took a deep breath for the looming ordeal. Honey, her arms protectively around both sons, followed Grace. Bob, Toppy and Doris brought up the rear.

The inside of the house was even more intimidating than the outside. The boys found themselves in a large, dark entrance hall with expanses of spotlessly shining wood floors, surrounded by fine ornaments that cried out, "Touch me not, on pain of death!" Straight from a cozy apartment over a store, Hub and Fat were cowed.

For a moment, they were all observed by May Bailey from her vantage point halfway down the stairs, her imperial pose in no way betraying the fact that she had just been straining to hear the conversation outside her front door. The elder Mrs. Bailey was a stout woman, ramrod straight with thick, wavy gray hair disciplined into a bun. When she began to descend, with the help of a silver-headed cane, she moved the way a large ocean liner moved, expecting all lesser craft to scurry out of the way. There could be no doubt at all that she was the matriarch of the Bailey family—and its absolute ruler.

When May reached the bottom of the stairs, she stopped on the last step, her face carefully set, making no attempt at physical contact with Jack or his family.

"Jack, I hope you had a pleasant drive," she began, as though it had been days, not years, since she had last seen her son.

Jack's face was so tense that the muscles stood out in his jaw. Nevertheless, he was determined to do his part. "You look wonderful," he returned.

May looked him critically up and down, seeing his bony frame and the dark smudges of worry under his eyes. "I can't say the same for you."

"I'm just tired."

"I'm sure you haven't been eating properly." Though it was hard to eat properly when you were bankrupt, the message implied that Honey likely had no idea how to feed a Bailey man.

"Hello, Mrs. Bailey." Honey spoke up, trying to start off on the right foot.

"Honey." May acknowledged her coldly and

reluctantly. "Here you are with the entire brood." May peered closely at the little girl clinging to Honey's neck. "This must be Violet. She doesn't look like our side at all. And these," May turned her attention to the boys, "are the young men."

Hub and Fat were literally struck dumb by fear.

"Hub, Fat, say hello," Jack urged.

The boys stepped forward an inch or two.

"Jack, those are not Christian names. You know I don't approve of nicknames for children."

"I don't see why not, Mother Bailey," Toppy cut in. "I've been called Toppy since I was a baby."

"Hardly something to crow about. How are you, Hubert?"

Hub had some trouble finding his tongue. "Fine, ma'am."

A glimmer of tart humor appeared for a moment, showing that May was quite aware of the effect she produced. She lifted one finely penciled brow and looked down her nose at the boys.

"I've been known to bite on occasion but usually not in the first five minutes." She sniffed the air. "Did somebody have an accident along the way?"

"They upchucked in our new car, Grandmother," Doris reported in scandalized tones.

"Jack, there are some old shirts in the bottom

drawer in your bedroom. I trust you haven't forgotten where that is. Clean up the children. And don't keep us waiting. Dinner is getting ice cold."

"We really weren't planning to stay for dinner," Jack attempted. " I thought we'd just push right on to the lake."

"Jack, you're staying. Don't just stand there. Clean up the children."

Strong man that he was, Jack bowed obediently to the sheer force of his mother's personality.

They all ended up at dinner, the boys scrubbed clean and decked out in shirts several sizes too large. The great dining table had been set with good china, on the lace tablecloth, with embroidered napkins in silver napkin rings and cutlery that, from its weight and sheen, proclaimed itself sterling silver too. A platter of vegetables and a bowl of mashed potatoes steamed temptingly. Edna, the young woman who "helped" at the Bailey house, brought out a platter of roast beef.

"I'll say grace, Grandmother," Doris volunteered, longing to be the center of attention.

"Oh no," said May. "Hubert is visiting. He will do the honors, won't you, Hubert?"

Hub gulped and mumbled something nobody, including himself, could make out.

May regarded him sternly. "Hubert, has no one taught you to say grace properly?"

"Mother, can we just eat, please?" Jack interjected, trying to avert an incident.

"Cans are for sardines," was her answer. Matters of grammar and deportment never left May Bailey's mind.

Bob jumped into the breech. "Dear Lord, forgive us for we know not what we eat, but we'll take a chance. Shall I carve, Mother?"

"Yes, thank you." May cast a reproving frown at Bob as the boys giggled.

Bob's grin as much as said to Jack, "I can joke with our mother and you can't." He set to work with a flourish.

"Well boys, now you just wait till you get a taste of your grandma's roast beef and mashed potatoes. That's for you, Jacko." He flipped a hefty slice onto Jack's plate. "This is for you, Hubert old boy. And this delicious piece is for King Henry the First."

The boys hadn't been this close to a roast of beef since long before the hardware store went bankrupt. The delicious smell and the succulent juices made their mouths water. What's more, they were famished. Forgetting all else, they tore into the rare treat with gusto.

"Boys!"

The staccato reproof came from the head of the table. Hub and Fat stopped, forkfuls of beef halfway to their mouths, and found themselves the focus of disapproving stares from all around the table. They had begun to eat before everyone else was served, a cardinal sin in May Bailey's house. Toppy looked as though she had expected as much, and Doris was freshly scandalized.

"No matter what you may be used to at home," their grandmother told them, "you can't act like savages here. Please have the goodness to restrain yourselves until everyone is ready to begin their meal."

This was the second slur on their upbringing—and thus on Honey. Jack wouldn't stand for it. "Leave them alone, Mother. They've had a long, tough day. I'm glad to see they've still got their appetites."

"All the more reason to display some civility. As the twig is bent, so grows the tree."

Doris giggled under her breath, a sound that stood out against the silence. Hub colored hotly. His fork moved, dripping gravy onto the snowy lace tablecloth.

"Oh good Lord!" May spluttered. "Grace, get a cloth immediately. We're going to have to put the boys in the kitchen if this goes on."

"Don't make a federal case out of a couple of spots!" Jack retorted.

Hub and Fat stared at their mother, frightened by the tension now crackling in the air.

"Please, Jack, let's not get into it," Honey broke in, desperate to keep the peace. "I'll wipe up the gravy."

"Grace will get a cloth," May repeated, with enough heavy authority to keep Honey in her chair.

Grace was the one who was scrambling up while Jack felt like tearing out his hair. This wasn't about gravy. It was about his mother's inflexible views and unyielding control over every aspect of the lives around her. And underneath that was strongly implied criticism of how Honey. had raised the children.

"For Pete's sake!" Jack seethed.

May regarded her wayward son unwaveringly across the floral centerpiece. "If you have any objection to the rules here, you may leave the table. You didn't really want to be here from the start."

"No, I didn't!"

"Grace, give Jack the keys to the house at Bass Lake. It appears he isn't comfortable here."

"Nothing's changed in your bloody house,"

Jack exploded. "Not an ol' darn thing!" He shoved his chair back so hard it almost fell over. "Let's go, let's go!" he ordered his family.

"Jack ..." Honey pleaded.

"LET'S GO!"

Hurriedly, Honey thanked May for her hospitality. May stared straight ahead without flinching as Honey quickly shepherded the boys out after her husband. They left Bob red-faced while Doris gloated and May went on calmly eating.

Grace ran after her brother with the keys. Outside, she fought back tears as Honey and the kids piled into the old truck.

"I was so looking forward to visiting with the children."

"Come out to the lake and see them," Jack invited, "any time."

Grace shook her head. "She won't let me go, Jack." She adored her older brother and had missed him terribly, but she had little nerve to defy her mother.

Ruefully, Jack kissed Grace on the cheek and hugged her as he hurried into the truck where his family was waiting.

"Drive carefully," was all she could call after them as the truck lurched to life and backed out of the driveway.

CHAPTER SIX

Despite the spat at the dinner table, spirits could not help but lift as the family found itself on its own again. The truck rattled along country roads until the glimmer of a blue lake showed up ahead and they drove up to an old summer house. Jack, holding Violet, grabbed Honey's hand, pulling her out of the truck and along the path. Happy memories of coming here as a boy flooded back as Jack watched his own sons race ahead, as excited as only children can get on a summer's day on the shore of a beautiful lake.

"Hey boys," their father called after them, "that's Anderchuck's Mill across the way. And there, there's the old beaver dam where Bob and I used to play. We thought we were big shots then."

The air was fresh and sweet with the smell of wildflowers; the water glimmered and danced. Heartsick feelings seemed to drop away, allowing a resurgence of hope. Jack pulled Honey close to him. "At least we're safe here for a while."

Honey sighed, remembering the scene in the

house. "If this is going to work out, you're going to have to try to get along with her, Jack."

"How? I can't even stand looking at her."

"I'm the problem," lamented Honey. "If I were only more like Toppy ..."

"Oh, that birdbrain? God forbid. She and my mother. Treat my wife and kids like they're dirt and my brother sits there grinning like some bump on a log. 'Here you go, Jacko.' I tell you, one day I'm gonna knock his teeth straight down his throat."

Honey burst into a laugh. "I'll tell you what, Mr. Bailey. At least we're together, that's what counts." She looked around for the boys. "Hey, you guys, come on up here, come see the house."

Honey took Jack's hand. With Violet toddling alongside, the whole family headed for the small white house that had once been a farmhouse. Jack slipped the key into the door, which creaked and protested loudly as he pushed it open. He smiled at Honey as they stepped over the sill.

The burst of late-afternoon sunlight from the open door revealed a musty, dirty interior. The furniture was old and heavily moth-eaten. Cobwebs and dust coated everything and hung down from the corners in eerie festoons. The air smelled as though it hadn't circulated in a year. Honey hid her dismay with a sporting sigh.

"Well, a little water, some soap and a lot of elbow grease should set this straight. Com'ere, sweetie," she murmured, taking Violet from Fat.

Jack turned to the boys. "You know, fellas, there used to be a trapper who'd come here, and he'd hide his pelts."

"Jack ..." Honey knew there was much work ahead if they were to sleep there that night. "Can you show them later? Fat, come here and help me. Can you guys go outside and bring our things in?"

Jack only wanted the delight of showing his old boyhood haunts to his sons. Honey caught him trying to tiptoe out with Hub, an old baseball and mitt in hand.

"Jack! Will you stop playing and start pitching in? Honestly, you're worse than the kids!"

However, Honey was secretly delighted to see her husband happy again, so she could hardly object when Jack insisted on checking the garage with Hub to see whether his canoe was still there. With Violet in hand, she threw back the curtains, flung up the kitchen window and gazed out at the lake, allowing herself to think, for the first time, that this fresh start might work after all.

The canoe was still in the rafters where it had been stowed years ago. Nothing would do but that Jack and Hub must get it down at once.

"Your grandfather gave Bob and me this canoe," Jack told his son nostalgically. "We weren't much older than you. We would fish in that lake for hours."

"Can we go fishing right now, Dad?" Hub asked eagerly, looking out at the water and imagining pike and bass fighting at the end of his fishing line. There had been precious little time for fishing in North Bridge and no lake nearby.

It had been a long time since Jack had been able to have fun with his children. He grinned like a boy himself. "That's a brilliant idea. We'll just tell your mom we're catching dinner for tomorrow, okay?"

The two of them failed to notice where the bow of the canoe was swinging. It whacked a hanging hornet's nest violently on the side. The nest broke free, plunged to the ground and exploded. Instantly a swarm of furious hornets rose up and engulfed Jack.

Oblivious to this disaster, Honey was scrubbing the walls inside the house while Fat swept the floor. Violet sat contentedly at the table.

"Boy, I sure can understand now why you can't stand Grandma Bailey," Fat commented.

Honey stopped scrubbing. "Now look here, Fat, I didn't start out not liking her. She pushed me into it. But just remember, she did give us this place, so she can't be all that bad."

Before Fat could reply, they were both frozen by a horrible scream from Hub. Honey snatched up Violet, handed her to Fat and raced outside.

"MOM! HELP! HORNETS!"

"Oh my God!"

"Mom!" Hub shrieked again.

"Look after the baby," Honey ordered Fat as she raced to help her husband and son.

Hornets were swarming everywhere, attacking anything that moved. Jack was stung all over—in his mouth, his hair, all over his body—and he was gasping.

"Jack! Jack! Come in the house!"

Honey raced into the fray, desperately trying to help Hub while, at the same time, tearing away Jack's shirt, which was covered with hornets. Jack struggled, his chest heaving.

"Can't breathe," Jack gasped through everyone's screams. Allergic to stings, Jack's body was reacting violently. Even now the passages to his lungs were swelling shut.

"Hub! Help me!" Honey shouted urgently. "Fat, get your sister and get in the truck. Okay,

Jack, we'll get you there, don't worry. It's all right, don't worry! We're gonna take you to a doctor."

Hub was gaping at the horrendous reaction his father was having to the stings. Together, Honey and Hub dragged Jack to the truck and pushed him in. All of them piled in beside him, the baby shrieking at the top of her lungs and Fat terror-stricken. Honey struggled with the decrepit vehicle.

"Come on ... come on! Oh, please God ... please start. Please ..."

The motor coughed and sputtered to life and Honey lurched it into gear.

Jack, in Hub's arms, was slowly asphyxiating. His face was ashen and every sting was a grotesquely swelling welt. Honey, in tears, was trying not to become hysterical.

"Dad ... Dad ... breathe!" Hub shouted.

"Hold on, Jack!" begged Honey as Violet howled with fright and Fat huddled against the door.

But Jack gave a desperate gasp and fell heavily unconscious across Hub, who had been trying to hold him up.

"Mom ... Mom ... stop the truck!"

Honey tramped harder on the creaking accelerator, desperately trying to get to help, any kind of help, as fast as she could. She didn't stop until she had driven madly, as fast as the old truck would go, all the way back to the Bailey house, the only source of help she knew.

Yet had the old truck been able to fly, speed couldn't have saved Jack. Though Dr. Barlow came at a gallop, he was already far too late. Jack died of an allergic reaction to hornet stings, in spite of everything his frantic family and the doctor tried to do.

Night fell on a stark scene inside the Bailey kitchen. Jack's body was laid out on the long kitchen table, covered to the chest in one of May's best linen sheets.

When the doctor finally led Honey away, she was like a baby animal, stumbling along, a low moan escaping brokenly from her throat. May remained standing beside Jack's body, stony as a statue under the terrible blow that had just befallen her.

Out in the hallway, Hub and Fat huddled together in the shadows just beyond the kitchen door, which was open a crack. After the doctor brought their mother out, the boys tried to peer into the kitchen. They glimpsed their grandmother looming up beside the still shape that, only that afternoon, had been their laughing, energetic father.

"How come we can't see him?" Fat whimpered.

Honey hugged both her sons, who were devastated. "It's your grandmother's wish."

"I miss Dad," choked Hub. He'd never forget the shrill sound of angry hornets for as long as he lived.

"I know." Honey, chilled to the core of her heart, could barely realize what had just happened to her.

None of them noticed May, who had taken over command like a general in the heat of battle from the moment the truck had roared up. In the midst of all the screaming chaos, she was the one who had sent for the doctor, who had cut Jack's clothes away from the stings, who had organized ice-filled cloths to try to stop the swelling. None of her frantic efforts had worked.

Now the granite pose melted. Her hand reached out and brushed Jack's hair back from his forehead. If Honey had lost a husband, May had lost a son. Her eyes filled up with tears.

"Oh, Jack ..." she whispered brokenly, in a voice that could barely be heard.

CHAPTER SEVEN

News of Jack's death spread quickly through the community. As was the custom, the neighbors all came together to do what they could. On the day fixed for the funeral, the Bailey driveway and the street nearby were filled with cars. Friends came, the women laden with cakes and casseroles. Toppy and Doris stood at the door ushering in the visitors. Among the newcomers were Jack's cousin, Hugh, and his wife, Matilda.

Inside, in the parlor, Grandma Bailey, next to Bob, presided stiffly beside the closed casket, acknowledging respects as people filed past. She had assumed her stern public face again, the grief she had shown in the kitchen tightly closed up inside her breast. The black of her mourning dress was uncompromising. Even the jet beads at her neck seemed to glint with a forbidding light. Edna was glimpsed, handing Violet to Matilda. Doris peered curiously at the goings-on.

Hub and Fat, fixated on the casket, sat on either side of their mother. Beside them, Uncle Joe absently smoothed down Fat's cowlick. Joe had come up just as soon as he'd heard. All were deep in a state of shock.

May glanced at Honey and Joe. Fat's eyes met May's in a flinty stare. May leaned towards Hugh.

"Cousin Hugh, ask the boys to come and stand beside me."

Grace had brought Honey a glass of water, an excuse to fuss over her. Honey was too bewildered to protest as Hugh led her sons off to stand reluctantly beside May Bailey.

"Henry, stand here," May ordered, placing the boys to her satisfaction. These were Jack's boys— Bailey boys—and they had become enormously important in May's eyes.

When the clock struck the hour, May crossed to Honey.

"We are going to our church now," May announced. "You'll sit on the left-hand side with your brother. The boys will sit with me."

Honey roused herself in the midst of her deep shock. "They need to be with me!" she said fiercely.

Everyone turned to look. May opened her mouth to quash this, but something in Honey's voice stopped her cold. May, who never backed down, nodded stiffly and walked away.

The funeral passed in a blur, and soon Honey, Hub and Fat found themselves standing round the grave.

"'And behold, I am alive forever more, and I have the keys of hell and death,'" the minister intoned as the family filed past the casket.

May touched the coffin. Bob, deeply shaken, gave it a little rap, as though bidding his brother a final goodbye. Honey, unable to touch the polished wood, felt very faint. In fact, she felt so faint, she wavered visibly on her feet.

"Control yourself," May muttered, digging her fingers into Honey's arm to prevent a scene.

When Bob helped Honey away, she dissolved in his arms in a half-faint. Bob passed her on to Grace, who was beside herself as to how to handle the situation. May, whose stance was as immovable as the granite tombstones around her, regarded Honey's display with distaste. Behind them all stood Hub and Fat, lost, frightened and ignored.

That night the boys were put into the bedroom that had once belonged to their father and their Uncle Bob. It still had the wallpaper with the cowboys on it and two narrow beds with dark wooden headboards and quilts.

"I want him to come back, Hub," gulped Fat as the two of them slowly got ready for bed.

Hub, on the verge of tears himself, turned away. "I know. Me too."

Fat suddenly sat bolt upright on his bed, his face pale. "What if Mom got sick an' died. Who would take care of us?"

Hub's brow knotted at this unthinkable idea. "Uncle Joe, I guess."

"What if he died? Then what?"

"I guess," Hub got out slowly, "I'd be the man of the house."

"You'd take care of me?"

"Yeah, sure."

Fat mulled this over for a moment, trying hard to imagine Hub looking after him. He longed for his older brother to be kind to him.

"But Hub, you don't like me. You won't fight with me any more ... will ya?"

For the first time, Hub began to get an inkling of real adult responsibility. He shook his head, as close to saying he was sorry as he could come. "I promise, Fat."

Honey slipped into the room. Though dying inside, she was trying very hard to be strong for her sons. She averted her eyes from all the pictures of Jack as a boy decorating the walls, and from the balsa wood airplane Jack had once so carefully constructed, piece by piece, which now stood on the night table.

"Good night, sweetheart." Honey tucked in Hub. "You boys try and get some sleep now, okay?"

When she got to Fat, a sob escaped her throat. Fat slipped his arms around her in an attempt to reassure her. "You okay, Mom? We're okay, huh, Hub?"

Hub could only turn his head away, unable to bear the sight of his mother's misery.

"Oh Lord," breathed Honey, struggling to get a hold of herself, "we're gonna get through this thing. We are ... I've got big plans for us."

"I love you, Mom," was all Fat could manage.

"Go to sleep." Honey kissed him on the forehead and hurried out, hoping not to break down again in front of them.

Outside, Honey leaned against the wall to compose herself. May loomed up out of the shadows, her voice with an edge to it.

"Let me be brief! You are no longer welcome to stay at the house at Bass Lake. I suggest you look among your own relatives for charity."

For a moment, Honey simply blinked in incredulity. Then she had to scramble for every scrap of dignity she could muster. In spite of what she'd just said to the boys, she had given no real thought to the future.

"Don't worry. I would never even dream of living off the Baileys." Shock and anger seeped into her voice. "I thought I'd ..." she cast about for a plan, "I'd move back to North Bridge. Joe has a rooming house there. Until I can get a job."

May nodded stiffly. "I've arranged a meeting with Robert in the morning before breakfast. I would like you to attend. Did your brother stay over?"

"He camped out by the river." Joe Callaghan had not been invited to stay over in the grand Bailey house.

"He may attend if he wishes." Without waiting for a reply, May moved on down the hall to her own room, the only sign of the day's ordeal the heaviness with which she leaned on her cane.

Honey sank back against the wall again, her heart beating so hard it sounded like thunder in her own ears.

The next morning, Hub walked into the kitchen to find Toppy and Matilda lacing up Violet's shoes and tying her sunbonnet. Grace hovered nervously behind while Hugh paced impatiently near the door.

"This isn't right," Grace was protesting. Toppy and Matilda froze at the sight of Hub.

"Mom told me to watch Violet. What are you doing?"

They all looked as though they had been discovered committing grand larceny. Matilda cast a swift glance at Hugh. Hugh fumbled sheepishly for something to say before he came up with the totally unexpected.

"Come on, Hub, let's go outside and play catch with Fat."

Unable to refuse, Hub followed Hugh reluctantly out through the door, when all he really wanted to do was hover near the parlor, where he knew a momentous family meeting was in progress.

Half-drawn shades, in deference to the recent funeral, gave the parlor a gloomy aspect. May, seated in a throne-like wing chair, stared out the window, her mind seemingly elsewhere. Honey, gaunt and red-eyed, sat on the very hard sofa, next to Joe. Bob cleared his throat nervously, addressing himself to these two.

"Mother and I have given this every consideration, and no matter how you slice it—"

"You needn't concern yourselves about it,"

Honey cut in, looking fragile enough to shatter. "I don't want anything from either of you."

Bob hesitated until a sharp look from May prodded him to continue.

"Yes," said Bob. "Out of a sense of family duty, for the time being, the children can stay here in New Bedford, where they will have a stable home."

Honey was utterly taken aback. "Thank you very much but I would never leave my family, not under any circumstances."

Before Bob could open his mouth again, May spoke.

"I will not allow you to take the children away with you, and that is final."

"Thank you, Mrs. Bailey, but we are going to be just fine."

Honey still didn't understand the force of May's intention. May Bailey was a woman used to control, who had learned control the hard way. After her husband's death she had had to run the Bailey Silver Mine herself until Bob was old enough to take over. She had learned to deal with the toughest of men in the toughest of times. She had kept hold of the family assets in the face of ruthless competition, greedy bankers and underground disasters. It was due to her sheer bulldog tenacity that the mine, upon which nearly all of New Bedford depended, was still running and turning a profit. But the price she had paid was her flexibility. To give an inch among hard miners was to lose all. Such jackhammer tactics were very hard on those within her family circle.

May fixed Honey with a penetrating stare. "If you are ever going to get back on your feet and provide a decent home for the children, you'd better put your pride in your pocket and take some honest advice—leave them with those who have the means to care for them."

Honey sprang to her feet. "Sorry, Mrs. Bailey, but my children's welfare is my business."

"I will not stand by and watch you wreck my grandchildren's lives," May bit out as Honey began to head from the room.

"Come on, Joe, let's go," gritted Honey, wanting nothing more than to get out the door.

"You listen to me, young lady," May interjected. "The boys are staying here with me. The baby is going with Matilda and Cousin Hugh."

"Honey, think. This is for the best," added Bob, joining the fray again.

When Honey was almost to the corridor, Bob got rattled enough to block her way physically. Joe was stunned by this blatant move. Honey realized, with a chill, just how deadly serious her husband's relatives were.

"Oh, I gotta get out of here! Joe, come on!"

"Stay where you are, Mr. Callaghan!" ordered May, freezing Joe where he stood with her commanding voice. "Honey, you'll never be able to hold down a job and look after the children."

Honey spun furiously. "You're crazy! You lay a finger on my children and I'll get a lawyer."

May folded both hands calmly over the top of her cane. "You wouldn't want to go through such an experience. With no job and no money, you'd be declared an unfit mother. Any judge would send those children back to me so fast your head would spin."

Honey stared at Joe helplessly. Fear had replaced the anger in her eyes. May would actually go to court to get the boys.

"Lawyers cost a bundle," Joe muttered, looking ill and wanting to stop this before it could possibly get any worse. "Let's just settle this quietly. We'll get you a job. Maybe we can get the kids in a couple of weeks."

"No! No!" gasped Honey, turning to Bob with terror in her eyes.

"Nobody here is trying to hurt you or the children," soothed Bob, though he couldn't meet

Honey's look. "Matilda is a fine, loving woman. They don't have their own children. She will look after young Violet as if she were her own."

"I am doing you a favor. You may not see it now, but you will one day ... you'll thank me," declared May, unswerving in her chosen course of action. In her eyes, there was only one thing to do for the good of the children and she meant to do it.

With that, May turned away. Bob, sweating, scared and upset, hurriedly moved Honey outside the parlor. "It's only for a while," he argued. "You are going to get back on your feet and things will get better. Come on now, let's go tell the kids."

Somehow, they all ended up outside the front door. "Please," pleaded Bob, extending a hand to Honey.

"Get your hands off me!"

"Look, this isn't going to do any good."

Honey jerked fiercely away from Bob as they stepped from the veranda. The boys, far down the lawn, stopped playing ball, instantly sensing how upset their mother was. Honey sucked in a sharp breath to compose herself, then she turned to face May, who was in the doorway behind her. She looked May straight in the eye before May could shut the door.

"You are not going to do this to me. I am

coming back to get my kids. I know exactly what you're doing." Her anger blazed. "Just because you failed with Jack doesn't mean you're going to get a chance with my boys."

With that, Honey fled across the lawn to put her arms around her two bewildered sons.

Though she could feel May's piercing glance in her back, she would have been even more upset could she have heard the words May muttered under her breath before she left.

"You ruined my son's life just as surely as you trapped him into marrying you."

If it hadn't been for Honey, May believed, Jack would have been working for the mine, like his brother, at home with his family and far away from bankrupt hardware stores.

Honey had all she could do to stay calm as she knelt before her boys. Only her eyes showed her true despair.

"Boys," she began, "I want you to listen to me. Grandma Bailey and I, we had a talk, okay? And I have to go away. I don't know for how long. I have to go back to North Bridge ... to get a job ... so that I can afford ..." she faltered and then controlled herself, "... to look after us."

Dismay filled the faces of both boys. "You're leaving us?" Hub croaked.

Honey tried to draw them even closer. "Grandma Bailey offered to take good care of you ... just until I get things straightened."

Fat simply stared at his mother. Hub pushed her away and tore across the grassy lawn. "I hate you!" he shouted at her.

"Hub don't! Please Hub, don't! Please ..."

Honey caught up with Hub and tumbled with him to the grass for a moment before he got away. As Honey sank back on her knees, Fat rushed to her side. Helplessly, Honey held him in her arms.

Inside the house, Grace was so heartbroken over May's rough handling of Honey that she turned on her mother with uncharacteristic sharpness.

"Those poor boys. You couldn't have done worse if you'd tried."

"You stay out of this, Grace," May ordered. May was looking out the window. Seeing Honey clutching Fat, she let the curtain drop on the scene she had created.

Sooner than she imagined, Honey found herself waiting with Joe for the bus to North Bridge. She could hardly hold back the tears as she handed a hastily written list of instructions to Matilda and Hugh, who were taking turns holding Violet in their arms. The boys clung to her, still unable to understand why they must part.

"I made a list of things that she likes to eat," Honey told Matilda shakily. "I've been trying to get her off the bottle for a couple of weeks. There's a song that she likes—'Lavender Blue, dilly dilly.'" Honey's voice crumbled. "She likes that song."

The bus motor roared to life, drowning out the nursery rhyme. Joe guided his unsteady sister up the steps and onto the bus. "See you boys," he called out.

The bus door slammed. The vehicle lumbered away, and only then did the boys realize that their mother really was leaving them.

"Mom!" they yelled, racing vainly after the bus with tears streaming down their faces.

CHAPTER EIGHT

An oppressive hush hung over the parlor at the Bailey house. Hub and Fat, feeling discarded, sat on the sofa, while at their feet, Violet played quietly with a carpet fringe. Across the room, May, Bob and Toppy were carrying on a conference in hushed tones. May nodded agreement to something and left the room.

Fat leaned uneasily towards his brother. "Do you think Grandmother will let us call Mom? Just to see how she is?"

"I don't know, Fat." Hub's voice was flat

"When can we see her?"

"I don't know anything, Fat. Just ... just sit quiet, okay?"

Grace bustled in carrying a croquet set, determined to put a cheerful face on things. "Hey fellas, do you want to come outside with me?"

She ushered the boys out, casting an unhappy glance back at Bob, Toppy and Violet. She knew that the fate of the boys was soon to be decided, and there was nothing she could do.

Toppy spotted Doris in the hall, settling in to eavesdrop.

"Doris, you go play with your cousins. The grown-ups need to talk."

"Mother, really! I'm fourteen."

Toppy shot her daughter a don't-cross-me look.

Doris flounced out just as May returned, this time with Hugh and Matilda. May nodded towards Violet and smiled at Matilda. Matilda scooped Violet up, delighted.

"There's the little one! Come on, come to ... oh

dear ..." Matilda halted, slightly embarrassed. "I ... I don't know what to have her call me. Auntie Matilda, I suppose ..."

"Why not 'Mama'?" May suggested matter-of-factly. "Whatever you feel is suitable, Matilda."

This was too much even for Bob. "Mother, we at least have to give Honey enough time to get back on her feet. Legally speaking," he added hastily in response to May's stern expression.

"Robert, you know how I feel. I don't believe she's capable of bringing up my grandsons properly. One day, I want to see those boys run the Bailey Silver Mine." May was used to making very hard decisions for the general good of all, regardless of how much they pinched the individual.

Toppy looked at Bob, their worst fears confirmed. May Bailey meant to cut Honey out completely and take permanent possession of the boys for her own.

"Yes," insisted Bob, "but we at least have to give her time."

May smiled grimly. "Enough time and rope and that girl will hang herself. I can raise the two boys, but I don't have the energy to chase after a two-year-old girl. Toppy, help Hugh and Matilda pack up the baby's things."

Out on the lawn, a little later, May and Bob watched the croquet game in progress from big wooden lawn chairs. When Matilda, Toppy and Hugh finally came out of the house carrying Violet, the little girl was crying loudly for her mommy.

"Hub?" Bob called out. "Henry? Step lively. Cousins Hugh and Matilda are here to take away your little sister. Come on up to say goodbye."

Fat and Hub stared at Violet's screwed-up face.

"I don't see why you hafta take her," Hub objected. "My mom can take care of her, herself."

"Your mother's got troubles enough, Hub," Toppy tried to explain.

May gestured at the boys. "Give your sister a kiss, so Matilda and Hugh can be on their way."

Fat hesitated, then kissed the squirming child. Hub, determined not to capitulate in this abduction of his sister, turned pointedly and stalked away, leaving Matilda flushed with embarrassment.

Toppy walked off with Matilda, Hugh and the baby to the car. Bob stood beside May, watching Hub, whose every move radiated defiance.

"That one's got a mouth on him, doesn't he?" Bob commented.

"He is willful," May agreed, looking as though she would have to do something about that.

"He's a Bailey," muttered Grace as she went back to the game of croquet.

Doris was not taking kindly to playing croquet with the boys. In consequence, she was trying to grab every advantage she could get.

"This ground is uneven—I get an extra turn, don't I, Aunt Grace?"

"You do not!"

Doris took an extra turn anyway. Furious, and still full of turmoil over Violet, Hub kicked her ball into the delphiniums.

"Hub!" cried Grace.

"Go get that ball," Doris ordered. And her voice grew deadly when Hub didn't move. "I said, get it."

"Make me!"

"You rotten little beggar ...!"

Before Grace could stop them, Doris had pulled Hub into a headlock. She was half a head taller and two years older. Doris wrestled Hub down, then grabbed his head and pounded it into the ground. In an effort to escape, Hub swung his fist wildly sideways as hard as he could—and connected with the side of Doris's nose. Stunned, Doris reared back as blood trickled down.

"I'm bleeding," she screeched. "Now I'm really gonna get you, you nasty creep!"

"Leave him!" bellowed Fat, who charged at Doris and knocked her off Hub. As she rolled and squealed, Fat scrambled on top of her.

"Atta boy, Fat!" Hub yelled. "Sit on her!"

As Grace tried vainly to pull the kids apart, May, Toppy and Bob came charging down the yard to the rescue.

"Get off! Get off!" Bob ordered Fat angrily. He pointed towards the house. "Get in there!" The boys were banished to their room.

Hub hunched over the hot-air register, which carried sound from the kitchen upstairs quite nicely. Fat sat sullenly on the floor, his back against the wall.

"What do you think they'll do?" he asked, to which Hub could only shrug.

In the kitchen, May presided from a wooden chair. Bob stared out the window as a very worked-up Toppy held a tea towel full of ice chips to her daughter's nose.

"They attacked poor Doris!" Toppy huffed accusingly.

"You're making it sound worse than it was." Grace was the only one who had been there from start to finish.

"It's the Irish in them," continued Toppy, as if Grace hadn't spoken at all.

Grace countered gamely. "They lost their father, their mother is miles away in North Bridge!"

"Grace ..." May said in warning. Grace was coming very close to defending Honey.

Toppy looked down at the red spatters ruining the front of Doris's visiting dress and the bruise beginning to ornament the side of her nose. "They are wicked, wicked, wicked!"

"You've no feeling at all, Toppy!" Grace exploded.

"Enough! Both of you!" shouted May. "The boys did wrong and they are being punished. The truth is, Doris, you can be blessed annoying. I hope you learned something."

Toppy swelled up. "Doris? Well, I've never heard such nonsense—"

Bob shot Toppy a silencing look. He crossed to his mother and leaned over her.

"Obviously, there is a discipline problem here. It's only gonna get worse and you know it. Or have you forgotten, Mother, what it's like to have two young boys running through this house?"

"Don't lecture me, Robert."

"I am only saying," Bob continued bravely,

"those two boys are more than you and Grace can handle. Look how upset Grace is already."

Grace blew her nose loudly. "I'm not upset."

"That Hub is pure trouble," Bob declared with an air of great authority. "Unless those hellions settle down in short order and start fitting in—I'm afraid you're gonna have to separate them, Mother."

"Bob!" Grace exclaimed, appalled. "These are Jack's boys!"

Even Doris was struck by her father's grave determination. "We were just fighting ..." she backtracked, seeing the croquet scrap blowing up out of all proportion.

"I mean it, Mother," repeated Bob. "We'll split them up if that's what we have to do. They can go live with separate relations."

Every word was heard upstairs in the boys' room. Fat looked worriedly at Hub, who was now leaning against the wall, his jaw tightly clenched. The fact that May didn't answer only frightened them more. Fat crawled over to Hub, his young face etched with concern. Hub's expression hardened into one of determination.

"We gotta get out of here," he said. "Get back to Mom, and get Violet back."

"How?"

"I'll figure something out. Grandmother won't know what hit her."

CHAPTER NINE

The boys would have been more frightened still if they could have seen what their mother was going through.

Back in North Bridge, Honey had to live with her brother, Joe. Reeling from grief and loss, she found it hard to do anything but sit and stare out the window. She was sitting this way, in her old chenille robe, when Joe came storming in and flung down his receipt book.

"The bloody tenant on the ground floor skipped town and stiffed me for the rent while I was away at the funeral! I mean, how low can a beggar get? What am I going to tell them at the bank?"

Joe was carrying a mortgage on the building from which he had hoped, in better times, to make some money by renting out rooms. When the Depression hit, one of the first things tenants resorted to was skipping out without paying their rent.

"We have to get our hands on some dough," Joe said, raking his fingers back through his hair. "We both gotta get jobs this week." Joe paused, looking at Honey. "I hate to tell you this, Sis, but you're not looking so good."

Honey's face was taut with physical and emotional exhaustion. She had barely heard anything Joe said. "I didn't sleep much."

"Listen, I'll sleep on the cot. You take my bed tonight."

Honey turned to her brother, tears welling in her eyes. "Joe ... what am I gonna do?"

"Come on. You gotta pull yourself up. You can't think defeat. You start to slide and there's nowhere to go but down. I've seen hard times do it to lots of other people."

"I just want to die."

The words were a cry torn from deep inside Honey. Joe sat down facing her, knowing he could not let his sister succumb to despair.

"Fat lotta good you're gonna do your kids, six feet under. Come on, feeling sorry for yourself isn't gonna make you a living. You may have married a Bailey, but you're a Callaghan under it all. And Callaghans don't give up, not without a fight." Joe took Honey's face in his hands and pinched her cheeks affectionately.

Honey thought of her boys and of little Violet, now with Matilda and Hugh, perhaps already forgetting about her real family. Drawing a long, ragged breath she straightened with great effort. Joe was right. Sitting staring out the window would not get her children back together—or even feed her, as a matter of fact.

The next morning, Honey bravely set out to get a job. Since she had lots of experience from the hardware business, she tried the stores first. Quickly, she discovered that they were hanging on as precariously as Bailey's Hardware had. She was turned away at one after the other until she found herself in a shabby bakery at the far end of a run-down commercial street. A woman in baker's whites and a hair net escorted her to the door.

"I wish I could help you ... but we're not moving the same volume of cakes, pies or tarts no more." The first thing hard-up people stopped buying was desserts.

"I'll sweep up, I'll work long hours. I gotta get something," Honey insisted, not caring any more about sounding as desperate as she really was.

The woman shook her head sadly. "You don't understand."

"No, *you* don't understand," Honey cried

through frustrated tears. "They took my kids! If I don't get a job, I can't get them back ..."

"I am so sorry, Honey," the woman replied, moved but still helpless. "There is just nothing to do. We're a small operation." The baker read an all too familiar story in Honey's drawn face. "I don't have enough work to keep my own family busy."

Honey pulled herself together and nodded wearily. "I just ... I never thought I'd see the day when people would cut back on buying food."

"There's a lot of hard-luck cases. I feel for you."

Before she burst into tears altogether, Honey walked quickly off down the street. She was trying to hold back the wave of despair that was sweeping through her breast when, suddenly, a filthy-faced little girl was at her side holding out a battered tin cup.

"Spare change? Can ya help us?"

The child was as scrawny as a bunch of twigs. In a doorway behind her, the child's mother stared back with sunken eyes, cradling an infant against her. Honey's eyes met the woman's—and saw a spirit completely broken. A shudder penetrated right down to Honey's bones. There, but for the grace of God ...

"I ... I'm sorry," Honey stammered, knowing she didn't even have a penny to give. "I can't ..."

Honey hurried on, so preoccupied that she failed to notice Joe, in overalls, loading a ladder onto the back of a truck.

"Hey, Honey!" Joe called out

Relieved to escape, Honey dodged through traffic over to her brother.

"How's it going, Sis?"

"I've been better."

"Awww! Well, keep your chin up ... but hey, look me over!" He modeled the overalls. "Tim Bursey's got me a job painting a house. Guess I'll spring for the groceries this week."

Honey could only manage a frail smile. "I really appreciate everything you're doing for me."

"What am I supposed to do, put my sister out on the street? Go on, take a lie down."

But Honey had had a moment to catch her breath. Her head lifted. "No, I'm up, I'm out. I'm gonna get a job. I'm getting my kids back."

Honey set out once again, trying every place she could think of, even the local hospital. While a patient lay under a sheet racked by an awful cough, Honey looked pleadingly at the Matron.

"I've got a good strong back. I don't mind washing floors, I'll change soiled beds. I'll take any kind of work you have. Just anything ..."

The Matron shook her head at an entreaty she was hearing more and more often. The hospital was running on a shoestring too. "We're looking for volunteers to do that kind of work these days."

Over the next few days, Honey tramped North Bridge from one end to the other, asking, begging for work. As many another had found out before her, there was nothing to be had. Honey had to face the worst. She had no money and no means of support save Joe's charity. She was reduced to asking help from the town.

Dragging her feet, Honey forced herself up the stairs and into the office of the town clerk responsible for Relief. The clerk looked appraisingly at Honey's still presentable dress and hat. Honey was obviously not starving yet, and Relief money was as scarce as any other kind.

"The dole is meant for the hardest cases only."

"Honestly," Honey pleaded, "I don't have anything. I've looked for a job everywhere."

The clerk only gave Honey an impatient look. Honey had no idea of the kind of heart-rending tales this woman had to deal with all day.

"There's worse'n you. Next, please!"

Deeply humiliated, Honey had to make her

way out past bone-thin women and children, the elderly and the infirm.

When Joe came back to the rooming house, he found Honey on her knees in the hallway, scrubbing vigorously.

"Hey, hey, Honey, you don't need to do that."

"Yes, I do," Honey shot back. "If I don't do anything else, the least I can do is keep this rooming house clean—earn my keep." She attacked the floor with frenzied vigor. "The floor's gonna be clean, the tenants aren't going to know what hit it. You're gonna be able to eat off these floors."

Joe knelt down, his arm around his sister's shoulders. "Honey, come on, come on ... Honey, you're all in a panic ... you don't ..."

"Joe, I have to keep moving. I'm not going to be defeated. Tomorrow I'm gonna get myself a job. You just see if I don't."

Joe gave Honey an encouraging hug. When she disentangled herself, Honey attacked the floor again, determined to scrub and scrub until her self-respect came back.

CHAPTER TEN

Honey's one consolation came from knowing that, at the Bailey house, her boys had plenty to eat— even if they had to sit stiffly at May Bailey's table to get it. At that very moment, May was intoning grace before they began lunch.

"Amen," they all echoed as May nudged Fat's elbow off the table and Grace served him a plump dumpling.

"Give Henry another dumpling, Grace," May urged, with an eye to having large, strong grandsons to run the mine. "He has a good appetite."

Fat, being younger and more pliable than Hub, was already finding favor in May's eyes. Hub, however, was bigger and hungrier.

"You didn't bother to ask me," Hub grumbled as Grace added another dumpling to Fat's plate

"She thinks I need it more," answered Fat, digging in.

"Clam up, Fat."

May gave a sharp cough. Grace hesitated.

"You're not to call your brother Fat," May told Hub strictly. "It's hurtful and rude."

Grace passed Fat's plate to May, who ladled stew over the dumplings.

Hub was unrepentant. "Ever since he was a

baby, he's always fillin' his face. My mom shoulda nicknamed him Pig."

May glanced at Hub warningly. "His name is Henry. And that's what I want you to call him."

"Even my mom calls me Fat," Fat chipped in, having long ago accepted his lot.

At the mention of Honey, May's grip on Fat's plate tightened. "Well, your mother is a woman with some different ideas." To Grace, she couldn't help adding, "She is a grown woman who lets herself be called Honey."

"Why can't we go live with our mom?" Hub burst out. He realized perfectly well that he and Fat were at the Bailey house because May had ordered it so.

This was a subject May refused to get into. She handed Fat his plate, brimming with savory stew. "Henry, you certainly take after my family—your good, solid appetite is proof of that."

As she accepted the next plate, Hub's voice took on an edge. "Are you even listening? I said, why can't we—"

"I believe I was speaking, young man. I don't answer boys who speak rudely and forget their manners." May paused significantly, then landed a still heavier reprimand. "I haven't heard you utter a single polite phrase. You shouldn't take your stay here with me for granted. You'd better remember how lucky you are to be living here rather than in a slum—or an orphanage—and respect the hand that feeds you."

This blast of sharp reality killed any further outbursts. Hub's face fell and he lapsed into silence.

Hub's grim mood lasted until that evening, when he came across Fat in the hallway, opening up a box of peanuts. The ruins of two chocolate boxes lay nearby. Luxurious chocolate smears decorated Fat's mouth. Both boys were in their pajamas.

"What are you doing?" Hub demanded. "Where'd you get all this candy?"

Fat grinned like a fellow who'd just dug up pirate treasure. "She keeps 'em in the closet. She must have a real sweet tooth. Have a bite."

He tossed Hub a chocolate as his brother passed by on his way to their room.

Just then Fat heard Grace begin to speak in the parlor, where she sat with her mother reading a book.

"It's awfully quiet around here. My goodness, you'd never think there were two young boys in this house, would you? I bet there's something they'd like on the radio."

"I've asked the boys to stay in their room this evening, Grace."

"You what?" exclaimed Grace disbelievingly.

"I don't want them underfoot tonight. My nerves can't stand the noise."

Grace let out a whoosh of exasperation. "They're children, Mother. Children make noise. Let them come down."

"Let the boys be, Grace!" May ordered when Grace half rose as though to call them.

The arrival of the boys had already stirred up the staid house. Grace, for instance, had found within herself a new defiance. "We are trying to make a home for them here, not a prison!"

"Grace," May gritted warningly, "if you try to undermine my authority ..."

"What? What will you do?"

"This is my house, Grace!" May told her daughter with rising ire. "When you learn to make your own way in the world ... then feel free to make the rules."

Fat was now crouched at the bottom of the stairs, listening, even as he crammed his pockets with bonbons.

"Not a penny to your name, nor the head to manage it if you did have," May continued.

"How do you know?" Grace fired back. "I did

plan to have a career after high school." She was now so agitated she hiccuped. "You know I did."

Grace had a bright and fun-loving spirit, but she had never been a match for her mother's forceful personality. Up until now all her efforts at independence had crumbled in the face of May's disapproval.

"Yes, I know that you planned something, Grace," May answered disdainfully. Then, as Grace hiccuped again, "Now stop it before you become hysterical."

Whenever Grace became truly agitated, she began to hiccup. It had always been a source of great mortification for her.

"I am not ..." Grace choked out over more hiccups, "hysterical."

It was too hard for Grace to maintain outrage when she convulsed every few seconds. As she deflated from the sheer indignity of it, May grew dismissive. "Oh, Grace, please. Now why don't you go upstairs and read for a while."

Fat hastily scampered away as Grace charged up the stairs.

"And don't interfere with those boys," May called up after her retreating daughter.

Grace had no intention of obeying. She went straight to the room where both boys now were and tapped on the door. Fat hastily stuffed a bonbon into his mouth and shoved the wrapper under the pillow. Hub lay on his own bed reading the funny papers.

Grace entered determinedly. Though she had regained much of her composure, she spoke in a prudent whisper.

"Hey fellas ... feel like a game of Parcheesi or something?"

Fat was trying to swallow surreptitiously. Hub didn't even look up.

"No thanks."

"Well, we have other games," Grace continued, trying to sound enthusiastic. ""We've got crokinole and Chinese Checkers. I'm sure we could dig them up, if you wanted to help me poke around the attic."

"Don't bother," muttered Hub, determined not to yield an inch.

Grace let out a breath. "Come on guys, give me a chance. I'm not Mother. I wanna be your friend."

Still smarting from the snub he'd been dealt at lunch, Hub refused to be moved. "We hardly even know you."

Grace crossed to the window, nostalgically harking back to when this room had last harbored spirited boys.

"Your dad and Uncle Bob hated being cooped up in here, you know. They used to do anything they could to get out of here and run wild."

Grace had hit on the one subject that riveted both boys.

"They did?" breathed Fat

"Uh-huh, and half the time Mother never even caught on. They used that tree to climb down to freedom." Grace couldn't help smiling. "Of course, it was a little easier before Mother sawed off all of the branches on this side of the house. Occasionally she'd catch on—a sixth sense she had."

Grace paused, perhaps thinking of all the avenues of escape that had been cut off for herself. "You don't know what it's like to be locked away here for thirty years," she sighed, mostly to herself.

Fat was already viewing his Aunt Grace with new eyes. Sensing an ally, he felt himself warming to her. Maybe she was stuck here as much as he and Hub were.

"How come you aren't married?" he asked, catching Grace off guard.

"Oh, nobody wanted me badly enough, I guess."

"Oh baloney." Fat didn't believe that for a minute. Grace, with her impish eyes and wavy chestnut hair, looked positively entrancing to him.

"Well, maybe one. Once." Grace quickly dismissed the thought. "But that's a long, sad story. Anyway, it's not so bad here. You just have to learn to get around Mother."

"How'd you mean?" Hub was unable to conceive of such a thing.

Grace sat down on the bed beside Hub and Fat hopped up beside her. She spoke in a conspiratorial tone.

"Well, you know what I do? I take the money she gives me for the groceries and whatever's left over, I buy something wicked for myself. Like a movie magazine, or a little bottle of eau de cologne ... chocolates, nuts ... I love candy. I know it isn't much, but ... it's the little victories that keep you going ... till the right thing comes along."

Hub and Fat looked at each other, realization dawning.

"You mean those boxes in the closet are yours?" Fat inquired guiltily.

"He ate them all," contributed his brother.

Grace laughed, a little embarrassed about her secret hoard. "Oh, that's okay ... just don't let Mother know." She got up and crossed to the door. "So, if you change your mind about Chinese Checkers ... or if you want someone to talk to ... I'm just down the hall."

After she was gone, Fat regarded the door thoughtfully. "You know," he admitted, "I kinda like her."

Hub gave him a brotherly shove. "Go sit on your own bed." Determined not to be won over so easily, Hub flopped back down to read his funny papers. Hub was trying to live up to his new, grown-up responsibility to take care of Fat, but all the turmoil bubbling up inside him had to come out one way or another. Naturally enough, he ended up teasing his brother. The very next morning, Hub snatched up Fat's balsa wood model airplane, the one that had belonged to their dad, and dashed off with it. Fat pursued him to the dining room, where Hub dodged about the table.

"Hub!" Fat was yelling. "Give it to me, Hub! It's mine!"

"Get lost, ya little pip-squeak!"

Hub made a dash through the French doors leading to the corridor and flicked the lock behind him. Fat twisted at the handle.

"Open up, Hub! OPEN UP! Hub, it's mine!"

Fat kicked at the bottom of the door. One of the cut-glass panes popped out and shattered at his feet. In the deadly moment of silence that followed, Hub opened the door and surveyed the damage.

May was already thumping down the stairs. "Stop this unholy ruckus!" she sputtered. Then she halted with a small gasp at the sight of the broken glass.

"It wasn't my fault. It was Hub," Fat insisted, with the air of someone provoked beyond all reasonable self-control

"It was both your blessed faults," May exploded. "Your grandfather had these doors specially made. They were brought up here by train many years ago! And now look what you've done! I've a good mind to do as Robert says and split the pair of you up! Hubert, get a broom before someone cuts themselves."

Hub settled back on his heels, making no move.

"Did you hear me?" May repeated. "While you're under my roof, you will do as you're told!"

"I'm not staying under your roof!"

May's broad bosom heaved. "You're just like your father!"

Hub's scowl tightened, making him look very much indeed as his father must have looked at times like this. The sight infuriated May, who now shook her cane. "Do you want me to do as Robert says? If you don't straighten up, I will."

At the thought of being separated from his

brother, Hub's defiance flared.

"We're going to North Bridge. You can't keep us here. We're going back to our mom!"

Hub bolted past May up to his room, paying not the least heed to shouted orders for him to come back.

CHAPTER ELEVEN

Hub was allowed out of his room again, through Grace's intercession, only to help Grace on her weekly grocery expedition. When they finished shopping, Hub, Fat and Grace stopped outside Mabel's Café, the place where Grace made her secret purchases of candy and movie magazines.

Grace handed Hub the grocery bag. "You fellas cool your heels here. I'll just be a sec. I'll bring you both a sucker." Grace wanted to cheer up Hub, whose brooding silence showed he was far from reconciled to May Bailey and New Bedford.

Not far away, idling at the curb, was the bus to North Bridge. Hub watched as the last of the passengers got on and the luggage was loaded. He could not help but remember this same bus carrying his mother and Uncle Joe out of sight.

"Hey," exclaimed Fat, "is that the North Bridge Express?"

"If we could just get on there ..." said Hub, his voice giving away his longing. "If we could get a ticket somehow ..."

"How're we supposed to get a ticket?"

"We got to," breathed Hub. "We gotta get outta here."

Ticketless, the boys could only watch as the driver climbed aboard and the vehicle lumbered away from the curb.

When the bus pulled away, it revealed a truck on the other side of the street with "ANDERCHUK'S LUMBER" painted roughly on the door. Its driver trotted into the hardware store, leaving the engine running. Hub's eyes widened in recognition.

"Isn't that the guy from up at the lake?" Yarko Anderchuk ran the sawmill near the old summer house the Baileys had visited so briefly and so tragically.

Realization exploded in Hub's brain. This was it! Escape!

"Come on!" Hub dashed across the road, the groceries banging against his leg. He had already slung the grocery bag into the canvas-covered truck bed and hauled himself up by the time Fat arrived, panting.

"Hub, we can't ..."

"Gimme your hand."

"Hub ..."

Hub lugged Fat up over the tailgate and tumbled him inside. And just in time. Yarko Anderchuk was back in the cab again. The truck lurched away a moment before Grace came out of the café, holding her movie magazine and two suckers. In utter bewilderment, she looked around. Where were her groceries? Where were the boys!

The boys and the groceries were having a pretty rough ride as the truck left the potholes of the gravel road to turn up a logging trail that seemed to consist of nothing but rocks and ruts. As the truck had no springs, the boys were bounced about like beans in a bottle.

"How are we even supposed to get into the cottage?" Fat wanted to know.

"I'll get us in. We just gotta make sure that no one sees us. Okay?"

"This is nuts!" Besides getting bruised, Fat was also getting scared. He had never done anything this wild before.

"I'm just buying us time," Hub tried to explain over the thumping and crashing.

Eventually, the truck reached its destination—

the sawmill by the lake. Cautiously, Hub poked his head out to see Yarko occupied with unlatching and opening the gate. The boys scampered out of the back of the truck and huddled in the undergrowth, holding tight to the groceries. The truck drove into the sawmill compound.

"Okay, let's go." Hub began tramping through the thick ferns towards a path meandering into the woods.

Fat struggled after him. "You're sure this is the right way?"

Luckily, the path led them straight to the old house. Getting in, however, was harder than Hub had imagined. While he banged and strained at a window, Fat sat on the grass and ate a banana.

"We can't live on these few groceries forever ..." Fat warned.

"Not if we keep eating them."

"I thought we were supposed to go to North Bridge. How are we supposed to get there, I wanna know."

"Fat, pipe down," snapped Hub, straining harder at the window. "We'll get to North Bridge and we'll get Violet back, too. But first things first ... okay?"

Grabbing a stick, Hub tried to pry the window up.

"We gotta get some money so we can flag the bus at the end of the road. Most important thing is nobody finds out we're here. Right? NOBODY! Anybody catches us, Gramma Bailey'd separate us, sure as anything ..."

Hub gave the frame one powerful bash. The glass broke. Gingerly, he began breaking the rest of the jagged shards away.

"We can't make any money," argued Fat.

"Yes, we can."

"How're we supposed to?"

"Trapper lived in this place, remember?" Hub exclaimed. "We'll trap."

The two were so absorbed in getting into the cottage that a voice calling out, "Hello there," caught them completely off guard. They froze.

"Who's that?" Hub whispered.

Fat peered over his shoulder to see a man leaning on a paddle and waving at them.

"Some guy ... in a canoe down at the dock."

"Don't let him see you."

"He's looking right at me," declared Fat.

Since it was too late for concealment, Hub stepped out to look around the corner, pretending they weren't breaking into a locked-up house.

The man was in his mid thirties with amiable looks and an athletic build. With one hand he hung onto the edge of the dock, steadying his canoe.

"How you doin' boys?" he called out cheerfully. "How's life treating you?"

Hub padded to the dock, Fat tagging behind.

"Your mom and dad around?" the fellow asked.

"No."

"Well, my name's Max Sutton. I got my tent pitched down the shore there. I just didn't want anyone to think I was trespassing."

The boys squinted at him, saying nothing.

"So where are your folks?" Max inquired in a neighborly manner.

"Ummm ..." Hub had to think fast, "they're taking a nap."

Still the fellow would not leave. "What's your name?" he asked, balancing easily in the slender craft.

Hub hesitated, but managed not to be caught out. "I'm ... Pete. Uh, and he's ... Sam."

Max acknowledged them with a nod and surveyed the wooden house front. "You know, I heard this place was boarded up. I was hoping to ask your dad where the good fishing holes are around here."

"There aren't any," Fat blurted out.

This earned a quizzical look from Max. "Gee ...
I guess Bass Lake is kind of a misleading name,
then ..."

"They're out there," Hub supplied hurriedly.
"They just keep moving around ... umm. Right
now I think they're on the other side of the lake."

"Way over," Fat seconded staunchly, with a
sweep of his arm.

"Okay." Good-naturedly, Max back-paddled
from the dock. "You tell your parents I dropped by.
See you boys later."

Quaking from this very close call, Fat and Hub
watched Max paddle away across the still lake.

The mood in the Bailey home in New Bedford was
a far cry from the tranquillity of Bass Lake. Grace,
after a frantic search, was forced to confess the loss
of Hub and Fat to her mother. Wretchedly, she
nearly twisted the handle off her purse. May sat in
a wicker rocker on the porch.

"Tell me so I can understand," ordered May
sharply.

Grace started to hiccup, not knowing where to
begin. "Oh God," muttered May, exasperated. "I
left the boys waiting outside Mabel's Café when I
went in to buy that blessed magazine." She hiccuped yet louder. "And then I had to wait extra

long at the cash because the bus customers were paying for their coffee. And then Mr. Woo starts to wipe the counter ..."

"The bus?"

"Oh my gosh!" Grace clapped a hand to her mouth.

"Do you know what bus it was?"

"It was the North Bridge Express, I guess. Oh what if they were," she hiccuped again, "kidnapped? My God, just like the Lindbergh baby!"

In a famous incident not that long ago, the child of Charles Lindbergh had been taken and held for ransom—and later found dead.

"People in New Bedford are not kidnapped," May snorted. " It was that blessed woman!"

"What woman?"

"That Honey! Yes, that's what happened. She's come and taken them on the bus. She's stolen them."

"Why would Honey do that?" Grace asked through more hiccups. "That doesn't make sense."

"Well, just what does make sense to you? Of course that's what's happened."

If May said it was so then it must be so. "Well, what will we do?" quavered Grace, caving in.

"You're going to North Bridge to bring them back."

"Me?" Grace hiccuped even harder. "Shouldn't ... shouldn't Bob go down and pick them up?"

"I don't need Robert gloating over us. We can handle two unruly boys. You will take the next bus."

"In the morning? Mother! I can't!" Grace was very nervous traveling by herself—and on such a mission!

"You're a grown woman. If two boys can take it, you can too!"

"But I don't know North Bridge and they do. I think we should call them ..."

May rapped her cane on the boards of the porch floor. "You are going to North Bridge and you will bring back those boys! Now hold your nose and drink a glass of water."

While Grace was battling hiccups, Hub was struggling to make a lasso out of some old clothesline. Fat gazed around at the musty rooms of the disused house, no doubt remembering their last, traumatic visit.

"This place gives me the creeps. It feels haunted."

"Ah, you're just imagining it. Dad told me all about the beaver pond where that old trapper who lived here used to trap. I think he said it was straight back of here. I figure we need about ten pelts or so to get enough money for bus fare to North Bridge."

"You gonna rope a beaver?" Fat asked, watching Hub's efforts skeptically.

Hub, who had no experience trapping, grew defensive.

"Well, if we can't find its lodge, then maybe we can just set a snare or something. We gotta trap them somehow."

Hub knew little about beavers and even less about fancy rope work. When he tried to lasso a can, he failed miserably.

Fat hooted. "I think to trap beavers, you need traps."

"We don't have any traps, do we, Fat!" Hub cried in frustration.

"Okay, okay!"

Hub returned to their problem. "We gotta make money somehow."

"I dunno how to skin a beaver, do you?"

"Well, we'll figure it out." Hub didn't even want to think of that messy job.

"Who'd buy beaver pelts from us anyway?"

"Well, as Mom says, where there's a will, there's a way." He tossed the snare and missed again. "Oh ... come on, let's go find that beaver pond, okay? Maybe we can spear one."

And that's how they ended up perched in a tree by the beaver pond with sharpened sticks for spears.

"How can you tell if it's a beaver or just mud?" Fat wanted to know, eyeing the murky waters just below.

"Shh, you'll scare them away."

Fat leaned over precariously. "Hey, I see a fish."

"Be quiet. We're not here to fish."

Fat was still staring downward. Sure that he saw a dark movement in the water, he suddenly threw his spear with all his might. He threw it with such force that he lost his balance in the tree and fell straight into the beaver pond.

"Fat!" cried Hub in alarm. But when Fat rose up out of the muddy water, drenched and sputtering, Hub couldn't help but laugh. "I'll get you. You okay?"

Luckily it was summer and Fat dried out quickly.

By nightfall they had to return to the cottage empty-handed. They managed to unearth enough moldy blankets for two makeshift bedrolls on the floor. Dinner was saltine crackers and cold beans from a can beside a paraffin candle flickering in a saucer. Hub scraped the last beans from the can into his mouth while Fat licked the lid.

"Hey, don't. You'll cut your tongue," Hub warned.

"I'm still hungry."

"Well, that's all you're getting. We're going on rations."

To emphasize this, Hub put the tin can aside and closed up the crackers. Two such mighty hunters might have to make Grace's bag of groceries last a good long time.

Disgruntled, Fat hunkered down into his bedroll. Blowing out the candle, Hub lay down too. Moonlight poured through the window but it didn't do much about the hulking shadows in all the corners. Fat began to chatter to allay his anxiety.

"What'll happen if Grandmother comes out here looking for us?"

"She won't."

"What if she does?" Fat persisted.

"We'll go hide in the bush."

Fat did not like that idea one bit. "People get lost in this bush, Hub. There's bears out there, too."

Hub didn't care if there were purple dinosaurs. "She's not taking us back, Fat, that's all there is to it. Now, lie down and go to sleep, okay?"

In the quiet, the night sounds of the bush crept

around them, including the strange, rusty gronk of the great blue heron and the even eerier hoot of the owl.

"Mom'll be worried," Fat began again. "Grand-mother's going to tell her that we ran away."

Hub lay staring at the ceiling and imagining Honey's reaction to such news. They would just have get to North Bridge before she found out. Meanwhile, Fat had been coming to his own con-clusions.

"We aren't gonna catch any beavers, are we, Hub?"

By now Hub had a lump in his throat. He couldn't think of anything to allay his brother's fears.

Fat began to cry. "How are we gonna get out of here? What are we gonna do?" he wailed.

Hub rolled onto his side and tugged his bedroll up around his chin. They heard small claws outside on the steps, squirrels or raccoons—or bears. Fat looked at his brother through his tears, leaving Hub no choice but to try to hide the fact that he was just as scared as his brother.

"It's nothing," he managed gruffly. "Go to sleep and it'll go away."

It didn't go away. It got worse. The howling of wolves penetrated the darkness. Fat squirmed over to his brother.

"Hub, I'm really scared."

"It's okay. Grandmother's not getting us back. We're gonna be happy again," Hub assured him stoutly. "We're gonna be with our mom again."

Huddled close with Fat, Hub listened intently to the night sounds. Through the window there were only the stars glittering in the cold silence of space. To the two boys, the isolated cottage quickly became the loneliest place on earth.

CHAPTER TWELVE

The next morning, Grace found herself at the bus stop in front of Mabel's Café. She rummaged through her handbag while impatient travelers gathered around her.

"Ticket ... oh, come on ... where is it?" She patted her bosom to quell the bout of hiccups she could feel welling up.

"Gracie?" It was a man's voice.

Grace turned—and her heart skipped a beat. The man grinned.

"Hiya! You haven't forgotten me, have you? Judd Wainwright ... fourth form chemistry class."

Judd, about thirty-four, was several pounds

overweight and talked too loud for some, but he had a kind smile, and today his eyes were beaming with pleasure at the sight of Grace. He hauled the leather case of a pharmaceutical salesman. In his presence, Grace's pulse quickened.

"Sure Judd! I know you—oh my goodness, are you taking this bus?"

"I am."

Grace applied her balled-up hankie to the back of her neck as she cast about for something else to say. "Going to North Bridge, are you?" "Yeah, guess I would be. It *is* the Express."

"Of course. What a stupid thing. I get so tied up in knots when I travel."

"Well let me help you. Is that your ticket there?"

Deftly, he plucked the ticket from Grace's gaping handbag. Grace regarded him as though he were a magician.

"Why don't you sit with me?" Judd continued. "I'll look after you."

"Oh goodness, thank you, Judd," Grace gushed gratefully.

Judd took Grace's rumpled ticket and handed it to the driver. With a guilty look around, Grace boarded the bus with him, extremely grateful for his company.

Before she knew it, Grace had poured the story of her mission out to him. Then, as rocks and pine trees sped past the window, an awkward silence fell between the two.

"I don't know what I'm gonna say to her," Grace confessed. "Well, what can I say to her? I'll just have to say, 'Honey, I've come about the boys.' That's what Mother would say. I have to say it like I mean it."

Judd looked at her fondly. "Gee, it's great to see you out and about again. It's really been a while. I think about you a lot."

"Well, I don't know why you would," Grace exclaimed disbelievingly, trying without success to squelch a blush.

"No, I do, I do," Judd insisted heartily. "I'll never forget that time you didn't come to the graduation dance when I asked you. You never did get out enough."

He reached for Grace's hand, which she hastily withdrew.

"Well now, that's not true. I get out plenty. I garden a lot ... for the fresh air. It's not so good for the hands, though, because they get ... all rough and chafed and ..."

"Well, I got a sample in my case that'll clear that right up."

Before Grace could stop him, Judd had pulled down his case from the rack overhead and was rummaging around in it.

"So you're in the same line of sales, then?" Grace asked. "Ointments and such?"

"Oh yeah, this is my territory: North Bridge, New Bedford, Golden, Pinebury ... Aha!" Judd lit upon the desired tube. "Now gimme those hands."

Shyly, Grace surrendered her fingers. Judd began gently applying the hand cream.

"Well, that's ... soothing," Grace admitted, beginning to blush all the harder.

"You can keep the sample." Judd put it in her palm. "Here, have a medicated comb."

Grace accepted these gifts with a pleasure that turned her cheeks bright pink. "It's a wonder you never got married, Judd."

"A big old barrel like me? Who'd even be interested?"

"Oh, well ... plenty, I bet," Grace replied in a rush. "Besides, you're not so ... well ... you're just about right."

"Thanks," boomed Judd, mightily pleased.

Grace looked quickly away, unable to forget the daunting task at hand. "Oh criminy, what am I going to say to Honey? I ... I don't know ... I'll just say, 'Honey, I've come about the boys.' That's what

I'll say. And I'll just say it like that."

Grace stared at the passing trees, wondering how she would muster the intestinal fortitude to pry the two boys away from a fiercely protective mother.

In North Bridge, Judd walked Grace to the corner. To her, North Bridge was a city, and it made Grace more uncertain than ever. Judd pointed down the tree-lined row of two- and three-story working-class houses.

"Ah, okay, your address is that way. Sure you can find it?"

"Oh, yes ... no trouble." Grace was not the least bit sure at all.

Judd hesitated, torn. "I've got an important meeting. Otherwise, I'd see you there myself."

Grace began backing down the street, shooing Judd on his way. "No, you go, Judd. I'm fine ..."

"You sure?"

"Go, Judd. Go, go, go."

"Oh!" Now Judd was embarrassed.

Flustered, Grace backed straight into a garbage can.

"You okay?"

"I'm fine," Grace assured him, even more rattled still.

"Okay." With a smile, Judd tipped his hat and headed away.

Grace turned around, and walked into the garbage cans again. Finally collecting her raw nerves, she set out.

After much looking, Grace finally found the address and knocked on the door of Joe's apartment. Inside, Honey was cooking at the stove.

"Joe, can you get that please?" Honey called out.

A moment later, Grace walked into the kitchen. Honey blinked at her uncomprehendingly.

"Honey, I've come about the boys," Grace got out squeakily, having practiced all the way down the sidewalk.

Honey dropped her spatula with a clatter. "What's wrong with them? Grace, did something happen?"

Grace's jaw slowly dropped as she realized that her mother's assumption had been wrong.

"Oh no," she cried, a new sort of panic setting in. "Oh, good gracious ..." And Grace began to hiccup.

"Grace? What happened?" Honey demanded, frightened by the queerness of Grace's look. "Grace!"

"What's up?" Joe asked, surveying this curious scene. He had just strolled into the kitchen, newspaper under his arm.

When Grace began to lower herself into a chair, Honey grabbed her and shook her. "Where are the boys! You tell me and you tell me now! Grace!"

"I lost them. I lost them both!" Grace blurted through a storm of hiccups..

Honey's face became even more papery-white. "What do you mean—lost? How could you? Where are they?"

"I don't know. I don't know where the blazes they are!" Grace stammered, hating herself as Honey stared back at her, eyes brimming with fear. Then Honey headed straight for the telephone and rang up New Bedford.

"Grace told me what happened!" Honey began to yell when May answered. "Where are my boys?"

"Now calm yourself down," said May into the receiver.

Honey had no intention of calming down. "If they get so much as a scratch on them it'll be you to blame!"

Silence traveled down the line as the truth sank in. Honey, May realized, shocked at last, did not have the boys!

"Now," raged Honey, "I'll stay put in case they show up. But I expect you to do everything in your power to find them. My children are all that I have left in this world. I will never forgive you for what you've done to my family."

CHAPTER THIRTEEN

No one could have been more grateful for the dawn than Fat. He had survived the terrors of the night. When he stepped outside, hope began to return. He faced a clear, quiet morning with not a ravening bear in sight. On Hub's orders, he made his way to the end of the dock and dipped a pail into the water. The whine of saws from the nearby mill cut the air, their monotonous drone almost soothing to his jangled nerves. But just as he was straightening up, a voice from behind startled him mightily.

"Morning, Sam!"

Fat spun around to see Max Sutton paddling up in his canoe. He had a string of fish, his morning's catch. "Your parents around now?" Max inquired, smiling.

"No. They ... had to go to town," said Fat,

thinking fast for once in his life. "To ... get something."

"Oh." Max paused. "I thought you people might like a nice trout lunch."

He held up a trout. The famished Fat visualized juicy fresh fish sizzling in the pan, and before he knew it, Max was in the kitchen filleting the trout while Hub and Fat looked on.

"So when did you say your mom and dad would be back?"

"Shouldn't be long now," Fat volunteered.

"I don't mind waiting a bit."

"Or they might be hours." Hub shot a withering look at his brother. "They said more like they'd be gone all afternoon."

Max neatly finished the fish. "Well ... I was hoping to have a word with your mom and dad. Actually, I was hoping to get a campsite out here if I could arrange it."

In fact, Max was taking in the squalor of the inside of the cottage: the bedrolls, the discarded tins, not to mention the disheveled state of the two boys. His lips pursed in concern.

"You and your folks really rough it, eh? Do you live in New Bedford?"

"Yes," said Hub.

"No," answered Fat at the same moment.

"Ah ... we just moved."

"Oh yeah?" Max stroked his chin thoughtfully. "Well, I run the boys' athletic program down at the school. Hey Sam, do you run any track?"

"No." Fat was determined not to get any more entangled than he already was.

"Well, if either of you ever want to come out and have some fun ..."

"Yeah, we'll see," stonewalled Hub, anxious to get rid of this keen-eyed fellow. "Anyway, you wanna get back to those fish while they're biting."

"Don't let us keep you," Fat seconded.

Reluctantly, Max headed towards the door. "Okay. Well, take care of yourselves."

"We will."

"And, ah, say 'Hi' to your folks for me ... when you see them," he called, as he made his way down the path to the lake.

"I think he's starting to get suspicious," muttered Hub when Max was finally out of earshot.

Hub was not far off the mark. Max was indeed more than a bit concerned. Instead of putting his fishing line back in the water, he paddled his canoe over to the sawmill and pulled up at the dock.

"Hey! Do you know who owns the place down the bay?" Max asked, passing the time of day with Yarko Anderchuk.

"Baileys. Yeah, a nice little place. Shame no one uses it any more."

"There's some lads there now."

"Oh?" Yarko Anderchuk pulled off his cap to wipe the sweat from his brow. "That must be Bob and Toppy out with their girl."

"Girl? Boys, you mean maybe? Two young lads about ten, twelve."

That stumped Yarko, who wiped his face again. "Over there? I wouldn't know who that would be."

After Max left, Yarko picked up the phone. "Mrs. Bailey?" Yarko yelled over the din of the huge saws. "It's Yarko Anderchuk from up at the mill. Did you know there was some boys up here at your place?"

Yarko could not see the anxiety draining out of May's face, quickly replaced by racing relief, then grim determination.

"I'll be on my way," she told Yarko, and hung up. A few minutes later, she was pulling on her gloves and climbing into her car.

Outside the cottage, Hub finished cleaning the fish Max had given them. Fat was making a pathetic attempt to split kindling against a stump in the yard. At the rate Fat was going, they'd never get a fire going to fry the fish.

"Here." Hub took the ax. "Let me have a go at that."

Hub took a mighty swing at the chunk of wood precariously balanced on the stump. The wood twisted sideways, sending the ax whistling down to catch Hub on the shin. He yowled in pain and clutched his leg.

Fat reacted in horror. "Ahhh, Hub! Hub—you okay? Oh Hub."

Hub was certainly not all right. He had whacked himself hard, cutting himself deeply on the side of the leg. Fat helped Hub hobble into the cottage and sat him down on the dusty daybed. Blood was streaming down and both boys were in tears.

"I gotta get help," Fat blubbered, ready to bolt.

"No!" Hub sucked in a strangled breath and gritted his teeth. "Look, get me towels. Anything to stop the bleeding ..."

"Oh jeez ... oh jeez," Fat whimpered, tripping over himself in panic. The best he could find were some rags that might once have been towels, before years of being buried in grime and gnawed on by rats.

"Yeah, gimme those ..."

"No, they're too dirty." Fat pulled off his own shirt and applied it to Hub's wound. Hub cried out in pain.

"I can go to the sawmill." Fat was ready to run again. "I know the path."

"No! Stay here!" Above all, Hub didn't want them discovered.

"You need ..." Fat touched the wound and Hub shrieked in pain. "You need a doctor."

"No!" Hub insisted fiercely.

Hub checked the wound himself, feeling sick. The cut was deep, dangerous and throbbing with pain.

"If you don't do something, it's gonna get infected." Fat's shirt was already soaked with blood. They needed more dressings in a hurry. "What are we gonna use?"

Hub tried to think. "Get some wood. We'll boil some rags on the stove."

Fat scrambled into action, tearing out of the cottage and grabbing up the bit of kindling that Hub had managed to split. He was beyond noticing the observant Max Sutton, who was now casting his line not far away. Racing back inside, Fat searched in vain for some paper and stuffed the kindling into the stove. The matchbox contained only a few wooden matches. Fat struck them all, one after the other—and the kindling still refused to light.

Hub moaned and rocked as he pressed hard on the sopping shirt to stem the bleeding. After a frantic search, Fat found another box of matches and a can of turpentine. He began dumping turpentine into the stove. In his haste, it splattered all over the stove top. He set the can on the stove top and fumbled for the matches.

"Hurry up, Fat!" Hub urged desperately. "Just light it, will you ..."

Fat knew turpentine was flammable, but he didn't know it outdid gasoline.

Max Sutton paddled over to see what the boy had been so frantic about. He was just hauling his canoe up on the shore when he was startled by a loud bang, like a car backfiring or a shotgun blast. He whirled to see the kitchen window of the cottage filled with flame and black smoke pouring from every opening. Max cupped his hands and bellowed towards the sawmill.

"Fire! FIRE!"

Then he started at a dead run towards the cottage.

The sawmill crew came running at top speed. They were forming a bucket brigade under Yarko's direction when May Bailey drove up and stepped from her car, aghast.

"Henry ... Hubert," she gasped as she struggled towards the cottage, the long grass and burdocks snagging her stockings.

Max Sutton staggered back from the door holding his shirt over his nose and mouth. He couldn't see a thing through the dense smoke, but he sure could hear Hub and Fat yelling at the top of their lungs.

"Hurry up!" he shouted urgently to Anderchuk. "There's two kids in there!"

The men from the mill redoubled their efforts. Gulping a lungful of fresh air, Max put his head down and charged inside. He made out two figures through the smoke and fire surrounding the stove. Fat was struggling to drag Hub towards the door, both coughing and choking from smoke. Wasting no time, Max threw Hub over his shoulder and pushed Fat in front of him back out the door.

"Hub's hurt! Hub's hurt," Fat screeched as soon as he could breathe.

Max laid Hub on the ground. Fat slumped down nearby, his face blackened with smoke and soot. As the men from the mill got the fire under control, May crashed through the last of the weeds, not caring about the effect on her dress.

"Henry! Hubert!" she cried out in an anguished voice. Then she spotted the blood on Hub's leg. "My God! He's hurt!"

This was a crisis. May was built to deal with crises. "Get some mud from the lake bed," she commanded. "I'll make a poultice. Bring me a clean cloth."

Fat leapt to his feet. "Hub and me don't want nothing to do with you!" he croaked at May in tearful defiance. "When he gets better we're going back to our mom! You hear me?"

May was utterly taken aback by the virulence of Fat's hostility. "I hear you," she gritted back tightly.

Fat was not squelched. "If we have to walk back to North Bridge, we're gonna walk it. It's all your fault."

Max Sutton regarded May closely. Fat's determination had penetrated her stoniness, although she strained rigidly to maintain her composure. Max could see she was struggling as Fat sobbed.

Anderchuk brought a handful of mud and a fairly clean cloth—his handkerchief, fresh that morning—to May.

"There you are, ma'am."

"This'll make you feel better, Hubert." May went to work on Hub's leg. "It'll heal a lot quicker.

You're going to be fine."

A short time later, Max loaded Hub, his leg well bandaged, into the back of May's car. Hub grimaced but did not cry out.

"Wounds like that bleed profusely—they look worse than they are," May told him. "I've tended many an injured man in my day, Hubert, when doctors were scarcer than hen's teeth. You're going to be just fine."

In the wild early days of the silver mine, May had dealt with hair-raising accidents with only her own coolness and iron control to save the day.

"You're one tough young guy," Max said admiringly. "You a fast runner?" he asked, trying to distract Hub from the pain. "You look like you got the build for it. I'm starting a track and field program at the school. Look, if you're gonna be around New Bedford, why don't you stop by. You play basketball?"

"Yeah, a little," Hub admitted.

"Well good. You can come by, practice your basket shots while your leg's healing."

In spite of himself, Hub found himself warming to the man who had just saved him. Max pressed his advantage. "Get ready for the team in the fall? That sound good?"

"Yeah, maybe ..."

"Maybe's good." Max got a little smile out of Hub and knew he had cracked the boy's resistance.

May settled herself behind the wheel. "Mr. Sutton, we need to be getting on our way. Would you send my grandson, Henry, out at once?"

"Yes, Mrs. Bailey." Max winked at Hub. "Don't be a stranger, 'Pete.'"

CHAPTER FOURTEEN

The next morning, May sat in her dressing gown fixing her hair for church. Grace stood behind her, in her robe and pajamas, telling about her ordeal in North Bridge.

"If you could have seen Honey's face, Mother. That is about the worst thing I've ever had to go through in my life. No matter what you think, she's still their mother, and she loves those kids."

"Get yourself dressed, Grace, or we'll be late for church."

Grace crossed to the door but not without one last parting shot. "Never make me do anything like that ever again." She stormed out, leaving the door ajar.

May looked at her own reflection in her vanity mirror. She felt weary, older than her sixty-five years.

From the hall, Fat glimpsed her, slumped in her robe, the iron lady without her armor. May spotted him in the mirror.

"Don't spy on people, Henry. If you want to be useful, come in and help me make the bed. Go round to the other side." Together they straightened the sheets and pulled the covers tight. "We'll have to go up to the old house and salvage what we can."

"Yes, ma'am."

"Your grandfather loved that house. I want to take you boys out there more often. Your father always enjoyed it."

"Yeah, he told me," Fat said, unable to keep wistfulness and longing for his father from his voice.

Hub, on his way to breakfast, paused in the hallway outside.

"Did he?" May fluffed a pillow. "Sit down, Henry."

Fat considered his grandmother carefully. Instead of the invincible authoritarian, he now saw, to his surprise, a vulnerable old woman.

"Henry, I don't believe your mother's capable

of looking after you," May asserted, returning to the pillows.

This was too much for Hub, who marched in. "She can take care of us all right."

May had heard from Grace how tough things were for Honey. She gave Hub a long look, really seeing how much the upheavals in his life had affected the boy. In that one awful moment when she had first seen the fire, May remembered what it was like to be a mother and had understood the panic Honey felt.

"Be that as it may ... she is still your mother. And of course she wants to see you from time to time." May touched Fat's shoulder. "I suppose we'll have to do something about that."

Fat's face split into a huge grin. He could barely believe this change of fortune. He began straightening the bedspread with such vigor that May waved him to slow down.

Hub squelched his own surge of hope. He would believe things were different when he saw it.

That afternoon, Hub's spirits had revived enough that he thought he might just wander down to the school gym. Max Sutton was working up a sweat shooting baskets at the Boys' Athletic Club. After a while, he noticed Hub standing shyly by the door.

"Hey, Hub, it's good to see you!" Max boomed. "That leg's healing up fine. You know, your grandma didn't do a half-bad job."

Hub moved into the gym, still limping, and asked hesitantly about Max's sports group.

"Oh, the Athletic Club? The boys'll be back Tuesday—bright and early. You gonna maybe have a look?"

Hub cloaked his eagerness in a shrug.

"Great!" Max grinned with sincere enthusiasm. "Now that you're here, let's shoot a few. Come on."

Two weeks later, to Hub's almighty astonishment, his grandmother made good on her promise. Hub was still limping slightly as Grace helped him and Fat onto the bus. May was there to wave the travelers off.

"I'll telephone you when we get to North Bridge," Grace called back to her mother.

"Don't be wasteful. You'll be back on Sunday. I can live without the sound of your voice for two days."

Fat hung back, looking at May.

"Henry, you're holding up the works. What are you waiting for?"

"Well, aren't you gonna kiss me goodbye?"

It had been so long since anyone had demanded

a kiss from her that May was quite taken aback. "No!" she retorted automatically. A Bailey did not make public displays. But when the bus door closed and the vehicle pulled away, May stood alone, watching. After a long hesitation, she actually waved. And, as she turned for home, a very sharp observer might almost have said that the imperious Mrs. Bailey bore two spots of color on her cheeks from the very pleasure Fat's offered affection had provided.

The bus could hardly travel fast enough for the boys. When it finally arrived in North Bridge, they clambered out, just ahead of Grace, and galloped straight into Honey's open arms. Beside herself with joy, Honey engulfed them, kissing them repeatedly while Grace, smiling, hung back. Joe stood nearby, waiting his turn.

"Hello! Oh, my goodness, I've missed you two so much! Hub, how's your poor leg?"

Hub extracted himself from his mother's embrace but did not let go. "I didn't mean to hurt myself. I just wanted to get back to you ... and Grandma Bailey said we can come every two weeks."

"And we can stay overnight," Fat crowed. "Is that lucky, or what?"

"Well, it's a start," agreed Honey, unable to

stop smiling. "Right? Oh, I think our luck is about to change, you fellas! I do!"

Hub lit up all over. "How long do you think before we can live together?"

"And get Violet back," added Fat.

"Real soon, guys," Honey told them recklessly. "Real soon."

Joe reached into the melee to ruffle Hub's hair. "Hey, I got an ice box full of root beer back at the house! Who wants some?"

As Joe shepherded away his thirsty, rambunctious nephews, Honey faced a hesitant Grace.

"How are you doing?" Grace began, uncertain how Honey would react to her.

"I haven't got a job yet. But ... you know ..." Honey shrugged and Grace nodded.

"What caused your mother to have such a sudden change of heart?" Honey asked.

"Oh, who can say? Just when you think you know Mother, she does a complete about-face, and you realize you don't know her at all." Grace paused in a kind of apology. "But I think you're right. I think your luck is gonna change." She smiled hopefully at Honey.

Honey, who couldn't help but like Grace, gestured for her to come along. Arms linked, they followed Joe and the boys.

"Thanks!" said Honey. "I sure hope so."

Back at Joe's rooming house, Fat, Hub and Joe joyfully drank root beer in the most pleasant place they could find—the fire escape. Honey and Grace squeezed out to join them. Joe, feeling expansive, affected an Irish accent. "Well, me lads, as me old Dad would say ..."

"Oh yes?" laughed Honey.

"May the road always rise to meet your feet and may the wind be forever at your back."

"I'll drink to that!" chortled Fat.

They all clinked their glasses, together at last, and brimming with hope for the future.

WIND AT MY BACK

② NERVES OF STEEL

It's just not fair. Hub's good at everything—including all the sports that Fat finds impossible. So when Max Sutton, the local schoolteacher, puts together an athletic team to compete for the local Fall Fair's Human Pyramid Contest, Hub naturally is right in the thick of things. Who needs a runt like Fat around? But as the pyramid nears completion, everyone realizes that someone Fat's size is just what the team needs.

Now if only Hub and Fat could actually *get* to the fair in time for the contest. With Aunt Grace driving, you never know what's going to happen.

ISBN 0-00-648154-X
$5.99
trade paperback

HarperCollins*Publishers*Ltd

WIND AT MY BACK

③

MY DOG PAL

It's a dream come true for Hub and Fat: they have been entrusted to "dog-sit" Pal, the town's beloved collie. Grandmother Bailey even agreed! But trouble starts brewing when Pal is accused of terrorizing the next-door neighbor's prize-winning chickens. And things go from bad to worse when Grandmother Bailey's purse disappears and guess who looks like the culprit? Pal, of course. It's up to Hub and Fat to prove his innocence, or else...

ISBN 0-00-648159-0
$5.99
trade paperback

▤ HarperCollins*PublishersLtd*